Niall slid a la...
ring on her fi...

'I can't wear this th... ...y gasped.

'Sorry if it's not to your taste, but it's only for one night.'

Actually, the ring was beautiful. Holly toyed with the band on her finger.

'And the only reason you went along with this pretence,' Niall continued, 'was because you wanted to prove to me that age had improved you beyond all recognition.'

Holly went scarlet. How could he know? This man got more detestable with each passing second. I must have been totally blind as well as besotted when I was a silly teenager, she concluded wrathfully…

Kim Lawrence lives on a farm in rural Anglesey. She runs two miles daily and finds this an excellent opportunity to unwind and seek inspiration for her writing! It also helps her keep up with her husband, two active sons, and the various stray animals which have adopted them. Always a fanatical consumer of fiction, she is now equally enthusiastic about writing. She loves a happy ending!

Recent titles by the same author:

THE SEDUCTION SCHEME
MISTRESS BY MISTAKE
THE MISTRESS SCANDAL

THE ENGAGEMENT DEAL

BY
KIM LAWRENCE

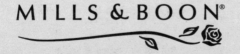

First published in Great Britain 2000
Harlequin Mills & Boon Limited,
Eton House, 18-24 Paradise Road, Richmond, Surrey TW9 1SR

© Kim Lawrence 2000

ISBN 0 263 82032 7

Set in Times Roman 10½ on 12 pt.
01-0011-53443

Printed and bound in Spain
by Litografia Rosés, S.A., Barcelona

CHAPTER ONE

HOLLY pulled the pillow over her head and tried to ignore the strident peal of her sister's doorbell. After several minutes of teeth-clenching determination to remain asleep, she rolled over onto her back and stuffed her fingers in her ears.

Whoever it was wasn't going away. With a defeated sigh, she threw the pillow over her head. As luck would have it, the feather-filled item managed to ricochet off the wall and knock a porcelain pig off her sister's cluttered dressing table.

Holly looked at the broken pieces and decided optimistically that with a bit of superglue it would be as good as new—always supposing it wasn't actually antique and valuable. You never knew with Rowena; her up-in-the-clouds flat was filled with an eclectic mish-mash of tacky but *fashionable* rubbish and staggeringly expensive items.

She looked around briefly for a robe. Although she'd moved in a week ago, she still hadn't had the opportunity to unpack her clothes. On reflection, she concluded that her pyjamas covered everything—if not more—that modesty demanded, and the style was unlikely to drive anyone on the doorstep mad with lust.

'Yes!' she snarled, opening the door a crack on its security chain.

'I need to speak to Rowena.'

You and about every other male under ninety in the city, if my sister's answering machine was anything to go by, Holly thought sourly. This was the first one that had got

past the building's tight security, though, so she assumed
that under normal circumstances he was a welcome visitor.

Holly brushed a heavy hank of dark copper-red hair
from her eyes. 'Well, she isn't…' she began impatiently,
wrinkling up her eyes against the light in the brightly il-
luminated communal hallway. 'Oh, it's you!' Disbelief
rushed through every inch of her, from her untidy red head
to her curling bare toes.

This wasn't how her dream went at all! A flicker of
annoyance crossed her face as she brushed aside the inane
thought.

Without thinking, she clicked free the bolt. Niall Wesley
wasn't the sort of man you left standing on a doorstep;
neither, she reflected, was he the sort of man usually to be
found on her doorstep. Beautiful men—and this adjective
was fully justified, in Niall's case—wearing dinner jackets
didn't as a rule come calling on her at eight o'clock in the
morning.

'Do I know…?' The beautiful, disturbingly electric-blue
eyes swept briefly over her diminutive figure, before illu-
mination dawned in those azure depths. 'Oh…Polly, isn't
it…?' Long-legged, and elegant down to his fingertips, he
walked past her into the bright open-plan living area.

I always knew I made a deep impression on him! And
it did a girl's confidence no end of good to have her sus-
picions confirmed, she decided wryly. She looked with
steadily growing resentment at the impressive rear view of
his broad-shouldered, lean-hipped figure silhouetted
against the full-height windows that ran the entire length
of one wall.

'Holly,' she corrected him coolly.

His smile was perfunctory and distinctly impatient as he
glanced around the room. 'Have you had an accident or
something?'

She'd completely forgotten about that! Holly's hand went automatically to her right eye. She winced and rushed over to a mirror; there were quite a few to choose from in the flat her sister called home.

She gulped. 'Or something,' she confirmed drily, surveying the damage. It could, she concluded with stubborn optimism, be a lot worse. Nothing too dramatic; a bit of make-up should disguise the worse of the damage.

'When will Rowena be back?' He glanced at the metal-banded watch on his wrist.

Some people might have registered the expensive brand of this accessory automatically, but Holly was much more aware of the fine dark hairs on his forearm briefly revealed by the impatient gesture. Her stomach gave an uncomfortable lurch. For heaven's sake, she thought in exasperation, anyone would think I'm still a silly infatuated teenager!

She suddenly remembered that intense adolescent vow she'd made the last time she'd seen him in the flesh—far too much flesh, as it happened, for her fragile peace of mind at the time!

The next time she saw Niall Wesley, she'd vowed, she'd have no trace of teenage acne, no braces and her hair would no longer be a violent show-stopping shade of red. The first two criteria had been filled, and she'd made the surprising discovery since those far-off days that some people—of the male variety—actually liked red hair!

She seemed to have some hazy recall that he'd be struck dumb by her stunning beauty and witty eloquence. A black eye and pyjamas that didn't even register on the seduction scale—and which, into the bargain, made her look like an undersized gnome—had not figured anywhere at all! This was what came of accepting hand-me-downs from a frugal

parent who was too polite to tell his elderly aunt that his
waistline had enlarged a little since he was sixteen!

At sixteen, Holly had nourished wild, foolish dreams,
but she'd grown out of them; reality was far too challenging and exciting—not to mention *exhausting*! All the same,
she knew that had she known she was going to see this
man, she'd have made an effort to look at her best. Which
means what? she pondered. A woman knew that even in
the twenty-first century, she would ultimately be judged
on her looks—was she vain? Either way, acknowledging
that her adolescent desire to impress this man hadn't entirely vanished made her frown with annoyance.

'I said, when will Rowena be back?'

Holly closed her half-open mouth with a snap. None of
the plagues she'd so viciously wished upon him had come
to pass, either. He hadn't grown short or fat and his head
was still covered by a lustrous, nicely trimmed dark
growth—the sort of hair a girl could really sink her fingers
into! Her cheeks flamed hotly as she imagined herself in
circumstances where sinking her fingers into his hair
would be almost obligatory. Her imagination definitely
needed a refresher course in obedience school!

'In six months.'

'What?' he yelped, his dark brows forming a firm line
of disapproval.

'Don't look at me like that.' She sniffed. 'It's not my
fault she didn't tell you.' She knew he had lovely manners;
he was clever, witty, in a slightly cruel way. He walked
into a room and people en masse fell under his spell. It
only seems to be me, she thought, that can see past the
high-voltage charisma and observe what a selfish, smug
jerk he is. Although it seemed likely his ex-wife had
caught on eventually, hence the *ex*!

'God, just when I need her and she's... Where is she?'

There he goes—me…me…me. The man's so egotistical! She watched him slump down into one of the massive leather sofas with a small derisive smile. Her smile faded; she knew with gut certainty that he'd slumped there before! Was it the only thing he—they'd—done there? she found herself wondering.

'New York.' With a gulp, she drew a firm curtain over her lurid imaginings. What her sister got up to with this man—or any other—in the privacy of her own home was none of Holly's business.

'That's it, then,' he said with a grim finality. With one hand pulling at the tie around his neck, he sank his head into the deeply padded headrest and closed his eyes.

'What's it?'

His dark eyelashes lifted and from the expression in his eyes Holly had the distinct impression he'd forgotten that she was there. Either that or he was just hoping she'd gone away so he could indulge in a bout of self-pity.

'I'm stitched up unless I can find a…' He shot her a sudden hopeful glance; by the time his quick once-over had reached her toes, he was already shaking his head.

'What are you doing here anyway, P…Holly?' Why, he wondered, would a grown woman choose to wear those hideous stripy pyjamas?

'The lease had run out on the flat I shared, and Rowena offered to let me hang my hat here until I get myself sorted.' Her new contract was only for six months; afterwards, who knew where she'd be?

Niall could recall some mention of the sister being a student. In fact, Rowena had regaled a dinner party with quaint second-hand stories of student penury—he remembered thinking at the time that it probably wasn't quite so amusing, up close—but all that had been a long time ago.

There were lots of young people with good degrees who didn't have a job. It sounded as if she was one of them.

He nodded without, she noticed indignantly, even pretending a scrap of interest in what she was doing in the present, future or for that matter what she had been doing since he'd last seen her almost ten years ago.

Ten years ago he'd been one of the select group of beautiful, brilliant people, including her sister, who had gravitated together at university. The charmed circle was how she'd always thought of them. Their glamorous lives had been equally charmed since they'd emerged to conquer the world, at least professionally—Niall wasn't the only one of the charmed circle to be divorced, though his had been the most public and visible failure. Served him right for marrying his trophy girlfriend.

'What's Rowena doing in New York?'

'The editor's job here is hers when Annabel moves onwards and upwards in six months. They want Rowena to…' Holly's slim shoulders lifted. 'I don't know what they actually want her to do,' she confessed. The inner workings of a glossy international fashion magazine were a closed book to her. 'But they want her over there, and they didn't hang around once they'd made up their mind.' Which obviously accounted for Niall's ignorance.

'We probably passed each other mid-Atlantic,' he mused. 'Good for Rowena.' Despite his words he still looked pretty gloomy about his friend's—did 'friend' cover their relationship?—success. Obviously he was more concerned about how it would inconvenience him! Thank goodness I don't have any friends like him, she decided with virtuous disapproval.

'I'm sure she'd have refused if she'd known of your dire need.'

Her sweet voice was acid laced. Niall shot her a sharp

look, and wasn't fooled by the round-eyed innocence of the sarcastic little witch! Yes, there was something of the witchy woman about her, with those big dark eyes and that wild hair.

'I'm very happy for Rowena. I know this is what she's been working for.' And scheming for, if he knew Rowena, he thought with affectionate admiration. She was a woman who knew exactly what she wanted from life and went for it. 'I'm just more unhappy for myself.'

'Yes, it must be so hard,' Holly commiserated gently. His eyes swept over her face, half-query, half-irritation in their depths. 'Being healthy...' —and that was some understatement; the man simply oozed a restless vitality— 'Rich, handsome...' She didn't even mention the stately pile and title that would be his when his father died.

Even though he was sitting down he managed to look down his nose at her, a distinctive masterful nose identical to those she'd seen on several of his ancestors' portraits. She'd seen the paintings that covered the walls of his family's ancestral home, Monksleigh Manor. She'd visited the house during its one open day a year—the one occasion mere mortals like herself were given the opportunity to drool over the accumulated wealth and history of the Wesley family.

'Thank you.' He smiled.

Holly felt suddenly less confident. On the whole, she preferred the snooty disdain to that heart-stopping grin.

'For what?' she wondered suspiciously.

'Handsome...?' One dark satanically slanted brow quirked.

Holly gave an exasperated sigh. 'Like you had no idea.'

He gave a modest shrug of his shoulders, but behind the cynical amusement in his eyes she thought she glimpsed something that was more weary acceptance. Did he find it hard to be judged by most people on his startling good looks? Holly dismissed this revolutionary idea with a frown. Who wouldn't like having conversations stop when they walked into a room?

'What did you want Rowena for, anyway?' She thought for a second he was going to tell her to mind her own business, but then his sensual lips twisted into a wry smile.

'Why not?' he said to nobody in particular. 'I was going to ask her to be my fiancée tonight.'

The breath whooshed out of her lungs in one noisy gasp and Holly plonked herself down on the nearest chair. 'You wanted to ask Rowena to marry you?' Under the circumstances, he was allowed to look a little piqued—at the very least!

'Did I say that?'

Holly, who had just started breathing again, felt her hackles rise when he looked at her as though she was incredibly dense. 'You said you wanted her to be your fiancée.'

'I've every intention of *never* getting married again. I only need a fiancée for tonight. The only halfway plausible reason for getting married, in my opinion, is to have a family—I've already got one, end of story.'

It was a plausible theory if you'd never seen the gorgeous Tara. 'You can't expect anyone to believe the only reason you married Tara was to have babies!' she hooted. She was no expert on male mental processes, but no man she'd ever come across looked at a supermodel and thought about babies.

'Although,' he conceded, choosing to loftily ignore her snide little interjection. 'Rowena is probably the only woman I'd even consider…' Knowing Rowena's opinion of the married state, he felt quite comfortable making a claim like this.

With shocked disgust, Holly recognised the knife twist in her guts as jealousy. She suddenly had a nauseating vision of herself in a dire frilly pink bridesmaid dress stumbling up the aisle behind the glowing vision of her sister. He might be an *ex*-fantasy figure, but she'd have to be a saint to be actually happy for her sister under these circumstances, and unhappily she was no saint.

'You're not making any sense.' Except with the bit about Rowena being the only woman he'd marry—he was being *very* clear there.

Had he asked, and been turned down? she wondered, her imagination now working in top gear. Rowena had some very inflexible ideas about a career and marriage and she often said that a girl couldn't have both if she wanted to succeed in either.

'You're just not listening. It's quite simple. I wanted Rowena to *pretend* to be my fiancée for tonight.' He carelessly flicked an invisible speck off his immaculate dark trousers.

'*Pretend?*' The man made it sound a completely normal suggestion. 'Why…?' She cleared her throat and continued before he could tell her it was none of her business. 'Do you drop in many mornings and make requests like that?'

The blue eyes lifted once more to her face. 'You did say…morning?'

'So…?' With a bolshy little glare, she got to her feet. The dignified action was spoilt somewhat by the fact she tripped over the overlong leg of her pyjama trousers. She half-expected to see him smirking when she shot him a dark warning glance, but he wasn't.

It occurred to Niall for the first time that the pyjamas that totally swamped her diminutive figure belonged, in fact, to a man. Somewhat bizarrely, the idea that she might have been sharing the bed in the adjoining room with a man shocked him.

He supposed he still had her fitted into the niche in his brain marked Rowena's baby sister, a funny intense little thing with braces. He checked...No, they were gone. There were other changes too, notably the clear creamy complexion. Niall suddenly felt depressingly past his prime.

'It's not morning.'

Disbelief showed in her heart-shaped face, closely followed by panic. He was in no position to judge; he'd had some pretty wild nights in his time, too.

'What day is this?' she asked after a small frozen pause.

Niall blinked. His hadn't been *that* wild! 'It's Wednesday evening.' He watched her sink weakly back down into the chair she'd just vacated.

'Are you serious?' she asked hoarsely.

'What day did you think it was?'

'I thought it was Tuesday morning.'

'It must have been some party.'

Even though a stunned Holly was still coming to terms with the fact she'd slept around the clock, and then some, she couldn't miss that definite austere note of disapproval in his deep voice.

'You sound like my mother.' It wasn't parties that her mother disapproved of, it was the hours that her younger daughter—as a newly qualified junior doctor—was expected to work. The farewell party after a straight sixty hours on call in the busy casualty department had probably not been a good idea. She had meant it as a joke when she'd laughingly said she was going to spend her fortnight's holiday sleeping!

'I hope you'll respect Rowena's property while you're staying here.' Niall suddenly had alarming visions of this girl and her equally wild friends trashing the place. 'Rowena does *know* you're staying here?'

Holly thought a little guiltily of the smashed pig. If only, she thought wistfully, he'd sounded this stuffy when I was sixteen, I'd never have lost a single night's sleep. Mind you, there was a certain novelty value to being regarded as a dangerous person.

'My secret's out: I'm a squatter!' She gave him a scathing look that would have shrivelled lesser mortals where they stood, or in this case sat. 'I need a drink. Don't worry, I mean coffee,' she added acidly.

'Feeling hung over?'

'No!' Holly glanced angrily over her shoulder.

She continued to futilely open cupboard doors in her search of a jar of coffee, aware that he followed her as if he was well used to treating the place like home. His next words confirmed his familiarity with his surroundings.

'The coffee's in here,' he informed her, reaching into an eye-level cupboard—well, eye level for him, anyway; she'd have needed a step ladder. 'Rowena always drinks the instant stuff.'

Holly, who had trouble finding time to eat, let alone brew proper coffee, snatched the jar from his unresisting hand. 'I haven't found my way around the kitchen yet. I've not actually been in that much.'

That he could believe. He watched as she filled a glass with water.

'Alcohol sends your electrolytes up the chute. That's why you're so thirsty.' Now I've started sounding like my father! Hell! What is it about this girl that brings out the stern parent in me? He hadn't forgotten the last time he'd had to step in to save her from her own stupidity—nor what he had got for his troubles!

'I don't need a lecture on physiology,' she told him

drily. Even if she hadn't read her books like the good student she had been, she'd had a wealth of practical evidence to back up the theory since she'd been working in Casualty. The gentle tap that had given her the black eye hadn't been the first time a drunk had got physical with her! This one had taken exception to her efforts to suture up his head wound.

'I take it black.' Holly regarded him blankly. 'Coffee: I take my coffee black, no sugar.'

'You're a very pushy person,' she told him, spooning granules into a second mug. If anyone had told me twenty-four—no, make that forty-eight hours ago, she corrected, that I'd be making coffee for Niall Wesley...! 'Why do you need a fiancée?' she asked, her curiosity greater at that moment than the growing desire to visit the bathroom.

'Just for the night.'

'Tonight I'm going to dinner with a woman who wants to marry me.'

Holly bit her quivering lower lip. His doom-laden announcement made her want to laugh out loud. She felt a spurt of unholy glee to see the roles of predator and victim apparently so neatly reversed.

'And you wanted to use Rowena as a shield.' She could instantly see where he was going; her sister was so drop-dead gorgeous that most women would be suitably intimidated. Hadn't she spent her entire adolescence being intimidated by her elder sister's perfection? 'How do you know she—this woman—wants to marry you?' This could be the arrogant assumption of a man who knew himself to be irresistible to the opposite sex.

'She told me.'

Holly's eyebrows shot up. The amorous female was not an advocate of the subtle approach, then. 'She might have been joking.'

Niall gave a dry laugh. 'Believe me, she wasn't,' he told her heavily.

'How can you be so…?'

'It's Tara.'

Holly dropped the milk carton and it spattered all over Rowena's stainless steel splashback. 'Not the same Tara…?' she asked hoarsely.

Niall had taken over the task of making the coffee as Holly seemed to have lost interest. 'The same one I married and divorced. The mother of my child…Yes, that's the one.'

'Gosh!'

'A more socially acceptable way of phrasing that instantly springs to my mind, but definitely…*Gosh.*'

'I thought she was living with that actor in—'

'*Was* is the right word. Now she's living wherever I happen to be,' he announced, in the voice of a man whose patience was wearing thin. 'I was in Paris, Tara appears; ditto in Los Angeles…'

'I'm sure she travels a great deal. Models do.'

'A book festival in Munich…?'

'Perhaps not,' Holly conceded.

'There's no perhaps about it.'

'Wasn't she the one who did the leaving?'

He nodded, noticing she'd seemed to relish reminding him of this fact. 'She's dripping remorse now. She wants to make it all up to me.'

He didn't sound exactly overjoyed at the prospect, but Holly wondered if this wasn't a matter of him protesting just a bit *too* much. She'd have thought the idea of Tara Steel, supermodel—she of the endless legs and gravity-defying ample bosom—making amends would have sent most males delirious with delight.

'Why don't you just tell her you don't want to marry

her…again?' It seemed to her that he was creating problems where there weren't any. Or perhaps this was all part
of a token resistance.

'I've tried, but she doesn't believe me, and I don't want
to hurt her,' he announced astonishingly. 'The press gave
the poor angel such a bad time when we split up, and when
I got custody of Thomas they got really vicious.' There
was no mistaking the warmth towards his ex-wife in his
voice. 'Sugar?' he enquired, spoon in hand.

Poor angel! Holly gaped at him incredulously. The way
the tabloids had told it—and, yes, she had read every single word—his model wife had dumped him when he'd quit
the glamorous Formula One circuit and left him literally
holding the baby! Did this mean he was still in love with
her…?

Heavens, she thought, aggravated by her fascination
with the state of his emotions, what's wrong with me? Two
minutes ago, I had him in love with Rowena. Anyone
would think I gave a damn.

He looked genuinely distracted as he absently stirred his
coffee. For once, he seemed to have forsaken his habitual
urbane poise. 'Tara is a woman on a mission,' he told her
in a tone of deep foreboding. 'She wants to rescue me from
a lonely, aimless existence.'

'Do you have a lonely, aimless existence?' she asked
unsympathetically. If he did, he only had himself to blame.

'Being single equates with lonely and aimless in Tara's
eyes.'

'My heart bleeds.' She stopped short of smirking out-
right—but only just. She widened her eyes innocently
when he shot a savage glare in her direction.

'I enjoy my single state.'

'Yes, I think I read something about that the other week
in the newspaper my fish and chips were wrapped up in.'

He'd been enjoying his single state in the back of a limousine with a young actress barely wearing a stunning outfit.

Annoyance flickered in his eyes as he bent his dark head in acknowledgement of her sly words. 'The awards ceremony debacle,' he said grimly. 'If I weren't a gentleman, I'd say the same thing to you that I did to that photographer. For your information, that stunt was a put-up job.' He ground his teeth as the little witch actually giggled.

'Of course it was,' she soothed. 'Couldn't you have asked—what was her name?—to help you out?' Holly bit her trembling lower lip. 'She looked to be a very obliging sort of girl,' she choked.

'No, I couldn't!' he bellowed. 'I never intended to actually produce a woman. I thought Tara would accept it when I told her I'd fallen in love.' He looked deeply frustrated by her lack of co-operation.

'You mean she doesn't take what you say at face value? How strange,' Holly puzzled.

'It just so happens I don't lie to Tara.'

Holly lifted her brows expressively.

'Normally,' he ground out, with an expression which suggested that throttling his interrogator would offer him the greatest satisfaction. 'I don't lie, but this is for her own good.'

'Not to mention yours.'

'I said I'd produce this woman thinking Rowena would step into the breach. That was before she vanished off the face of the earth. Now…Now I've got about—' he looked down at his watch '—about thirty minutes to find a stand-in lover.'

'I'd have thought there would have been a whole flock of lovelies gagging to help you out.'

He raised guileless blue eyes to her face and mournfully

nodded his agreement. 'The problem is,' he confided in a slow languid drawl that, had she known it, was pitched deliberately to aggravate her, 'they wouldn't all be as happy as Rowena to hand back the ring in the morning. I could well be jumping from the frying-pan into the fire.'

'God, it must be tough being irresistible!' Teeth clenched, she sighed sympathetically.

Niall gave her a long thoughtful look. 'I'd ask you to step into the breach...' He paused politely while she made a rude derogatory noise in her throat. 'But I get the impression you don't like me. Besides, you're not exactly...' With a pained expression he tactfully averted his eyes from her colourful striped pyjamas.

'Not exactly what?' she jumped in, bristling with suspicion. As if she needed to ask! He was implying, and not very subtly, that nobody would believe a man like him would want to marry a girl like her.

Holly's firm chin went up to an aggressive angle. She might not be every man's first choice, but to be deemed unworthy even to be the last choice of a *desperate* man...! Well, this wasn't the same little girl who had been reduced to abject misery by a careless cruel comment, and Niall Wesley was about to find that out. She'd show him!

'Not exactly dressed for the occasion.'

He was awfully glad he had dredged up a memory of Rowena saying that the best way to make her sister do anything was to tell her not to! 'She's so pig-headed it's unbelievable!' Rowena had informed him with affectionate irritation. She hadn't mentioned the size sixteen chip on Holly's size eight shoulder, though!

Holly wasn't going to let him wriggle out of this that easily. If he thought she wasn't good enough to be seen with him, he'd have to come out and say so!

'I've got other clothes and some people,' she taunted, 'think I scrub up quite well.'

'I'm sure they do,' he soothed smoothly. The gleam in his eyes made Holly frown as she suddenly felt less certain of what she was doing. 'Shouldn't you hurry?'

'Hurry?'

'If we're going to get to dinner on time.'

Holly's mouth opened and she blinked. 'Why would I want to help you? I didn't say I'd—'

'Well, if you don't think you're up to the task,' he drawled understandingly.

By this point Holly was ninety-nine per cent certain that she'd been manipulated by an expert, but a combination of that one per cent uncertainty and a congenital stubborn inability to back down from a challenge made her respond immediately.

'I draw the line at drooling over you.'

'Don't worry,' he soothed, his dark head inclining graciously, 'I can work around that.'

Stifling a grin, he watched her small stiff-backed figure retire to the bedroom, muttering ferociously under her breath.

Ten minutes later, as she emerged from a hot shower, Holly still wasn't quite sure how she'd got herself into this mess. She was even less sure why she felt excited. Wearing nothing but a towel wrapped turban-like around her head, she stalked back into the bedroom with the unconsciously smooth, graceful stride of a cat. She then opened the two neatly packed suitcases which contained a large proportion of her worldly goods.

Lips pursed, she extracted a few items and her eyes travelled to the full-length view of herself in the cherub-decorated cheval mirror set just behind her. Not too bad, she conceded, staring critically at the firm gentle curves that were in pleasing proportion to her diminutive frame. Not great, but not bad, she decided, holding up a bias-cut dove-grey silk dress against her slightly damp body. The creases in the long flowing gown made her frown. A spark of mischief entered her dark eyes.

Standing behind the door, she opened it a crack and flung out the dress. 'Be a lamb and iron it for me, if you don't want to be late!' she instructed loudly.

She closed the door with a firm click before he had an opportunity to reply. Well, I bet that'll be a first. Niall Wesley, former pin-up of the racing circuit, present boss of the family publishing empire and future titled lord of Monksleigh and several thousand acres…ironing…? The man had spent his life surrounded by flunkies—it was likely he hadn't learnt to tie his own shoelaces yet! She gave a small chuckle as she sat down to explore the Aladdin's cave of cosmetics on her sister's dressing table.

Her hair was still damp when, with a clever twist of her wrist, she secured the heavy copper swathe in a loose knot at the nape of her neck before pulling loose a few long soft curling tendrils to frame her face. She screwed up her nose in approval at the overall effect. Fortunately, the black eye had proved simple to disguise.

She sniffed at the neck of an interestingly shaped perfume spray before dousing her body in a generous mist of scent. All I need now, she thought, slipping on some underwear and then a pair of high-heeled mules, is the dress.

There was only pause enough between the light tap on the door and it swinging open for her to clamp her hands over her bare breasts and fix an indignant expression on her face.

Although she would have happily crawled out of her skin, pride made Holly stand immobile while his startling cerulean eyes travelled over her skimpily clad body from head to toe, pausing noticeably longer over some areas than others.

'You were right.'

One nicely shaped brow rose in haughty enquiry as she tried to maintain the illusion that she felt perfectly at ease with this nerve-shredding situation. Actually, until that moment she'd have claimed she was quite relaxed about her own body, only suddenly…She shivered, even though her skin felt hot. She felt conscious of every centimetre.

Calm down, Holly, she told herself. Niall Wesley has seen more beautiful women naked than you've had hot dinners, and you're only passable. Being passable didn't stop a violent surge of feeling rushing through her, a feeling that was purely sexual.

'You do scrub up well.' His sardonic mask left his words open to any interpretation she wished to place upon them—no, better by far not to think too much, if at all, about what he might mean! 'Here.' He held out the dress—which was draped across one arm—towards her.

'Thanks.' Automatically, she began to stretch out one hand towards him before realising how exposed, quite literally, this gesture left her. She gave a dismayed gasp and retracted her hand, but not before the erect coral tip of her exposed breast had peeked out. 'You'd better leave it on the bed,' Her voice cracked as she made a desperate attempt to regain her composure. 'Hurry up, will you?' she snapped as he strolled slowly towards the bed…Had he slept in it with Rowena? 'We don't want to keep your wife waiting.'

He laid the soft garment on the bed and smoothed it with the flat of his hand. The gesture brought a searing image to her head of the same hand stroking bare flesh.

He straightened up. 'Ex-wife,' he reminded her softly.

'And Tara's never been on time for anything in her life—even her own wedding, as I recall…So don't break your neck. There's no big rush.'

'Now he tells me.' She had managed to slide on a robe of Rowena's over her minuscule pants and hold-ups and she was able to sound more like herself.

That sensation had just been because she felt vulnerable—him being fully dressed and her being almost naked, she told herself comfortingly. Yes, that had a nice comfortingly logical sound to it, she decided, tying the sash of the pale green robe around her waist. If he'd been naked too he wouldn't have had the upper hand at all; they'd have been on more of an equal footing.

As images of Niall Wesley's well-built naked body flashed through her mind, her lovely little theory crumbled. Oh, God, she thought, as he turned to flash her the sort of smile that made her worry he had read her mind. I'll be glad when this night is over!

CHAPTER TWO

'THERE'S no time to think up a cover story so when we get there leave me to do most of the talking.' Businesslike, Niall cast her an arrogantly stern look.

'Laryngitis?' Holly queried meekly. 'Or am I meant to be struck dumb by my good fortune in landing you?'

He took her hand and, before she could protest, had slid a large flashy-looking sapphire ring on one finger. 'It's smart remarks like that I'm talking about,' he said, observing the effect of the large sparkling gem on her small slim finger with a critical frown.

'I can't wear this thing!' she gasped in tones of revulsion.

'Sorry if it's not to your taste, but it's only for one night.'

Not to my taste? Actually, it was beautiful and probably scarily expensive. 'It's too big, I might lose it,' she babbled, feeling her chest tighten as pure panic gripped her. It would probably have fitted Rowena like a glove—perhaps it had been made for her? This possibility made it even more imperative to rip it off her own finger.

'The setting's quite old-fashioned; Tara never wanted it. It was my grandmother's,' Niall announced casually.

Under the circumstances, it was perverse to feel as if she was wearing another woman's cast-offs. It was even more perverse to mind—but she did.

'I don't think your Tara is going to swallow this, Niall,' Holly remarked, staring at the heavy ring as if it were going to jump up and bite her.

25

'So long as you can withstand the odd cryptic dig, she'll believe it. Tara doesn't have a suspicious bone in her body. I've never lied to her before, so she has no reason to believe I've begun now.'

Holly toyed with the uncomfortable band on her finger. *'Never?'* she challenged sceptically.

'Never,' he confirmed firmly. 'If you discount the odd occasion when I've said I'd like nothing better than to spend my afternoon sitting in the front row of a catwalk show.'

'I'm just amazed this perfect, *honest* marriage ever broke up.' Holly gave a disgruntled sniff. He was painting a picture of himself as a remarkably devoted husband.

'It probably broke up when it did *because* it was so honest.'

For someone who accused her of making cryptic remarks, he produced the odd gem himself. 'Are you saying marriages stand a better chance of survival with a liberal sprinkling of deceit?'

'I'm saying I didn't want to stay married to a woman who was in love with someone else.'

'Oh!' His frankness was extremely unsettling. He didn't sound like a man whose ego had taken a beating, but perhaps that hard exterior was hiding a shattered heart? 'She's not in love with someone else now, though, is she?'

'Your thinking is predictably female.'

'I am female.'

'In that dress there was never any question about it, but then that was the object of the exercise wasn't it?'

'Pardon…?' Unfortunately he didn't seem to find her tone of haughty detachment much of a deterrent—not if his cynical smirk was anything to go by. Looking into those deep blue, *knowing* eyes made Holly wish she hadn't let vanity overcome her better judgement and agreed to go along with this silly scheme.

'The only reason you went along with this was because you wanted to prove to me that age had improved you beyond all recognition.'

Holly went scarlet. How, how could he know? 'That's—'

'Perfectly understandable for a person with an outsize chip on her shoulder.'

Holly gasped. This man got more *detestable* with each passing second. I must have been totally blind as well as besotted when I was a silly teenager she concluded wrathfully. 'I have not—'

'Whatever you say.' He waved aside her choked denial with languid disinterest. 'And actually, Tara *is* still in love with another man—the same man. Tara's carrying around a burden of guilt about leaving me and Thomas. It's that guilt that's stopping her from finding happiness. I care a lot about Tara and I want her to be happy.'

'Am I supposed to believe you're some sort of altruistic saint?'

'Frankly, I don't give that—' The pistol-crack of his long fingers indicated the depth of his disinterest '—about what you think about me. I'm just asking you to remember you've left your broomstick at home tonight.'

Broomstick? The cheek of the man! 'I'll be sweet and submissive, just the way you like it,' Holly agreed, all humble co-operation and saccharine smile. She'd never let a man do the talking for her throughout her entire adult life, and she had no intention of starting now! She swivelled slightly to look directly up at the big man who sat beside her in the taxi.

He was straightening the dark tie set against the brown column of his strong neck. The subdued light emphasised the sharp angles and planes of his intimidatingly handsome face but, after her silly gobsmacked behaviour in the bedroom, Holly wasn't about to be intimidated by his blue eyes and sexy mouth. She chose to ignore the sudden painful clenching of her disobedient stomach muscles.

Niall stopped what he was doing and slanted her a worryingly ambiguous look. 'You've absolutely no idea about "the way I like it".' The sensual gleam in his eyes as they rested on her defiant face caused more damage to her nervous system than an electrical storm.

Stubbornly, she didn't scuttle to the opposite corner of the taxi and hide her face in her hands like she wanted to. There ought to be a law about any one male wielding this much in-your-face masculine virility, she thought.

'I'll be hanging on your every word, darling,' she promised insincerely, batting her lashes at him.

'And for God's sake,' he warned, taking her provocative sarcasm in his stride, 'don't drink too much!'

Holly's mouth tightened as he threw a 'that's all I need' look in her direction. The righteous feeling of ill use swelled in her chest. He seemed to have conveniently forgotten that she, out of the goodness of her heart, was helping him out of a sticky situation.

'You're assuming I'm an indiscreet drunk.' Did two white wines make her a drunk? The way she recalled it, drinking wine after an exhausting weekend on call had made her extremely sleepy not the life and soul of the party.

'Well, if your eye is anything to go by, you're definitely a clumsy drunk.' He reached out towards her face but didn't make contact.

Holly closed her eyes, wondering what he was making of her instinctive and embarrassingly dramatic recoil from his extended hand. The shivery hot flesh of her bare shoulder was reacting as though his fingers had made contact.

'Actually, I didn't fall over.'

'Then how did you get it?'

'I was slow to duck...' His blank expression indicated Niall was a bit slow too...on the uptake, anyhow, so she casually elaborated. 'A fist did the damage,' she recalled ruefully.

He sat very still during the lengthy pause that followed her startling but matter of fact statement.

'A man did that to you?' There was icy distaste in his voice.

'It wasn't as bad as the last time,' Holly continued cheerfully, blissfully ignorant in the dim light of the growing shocked revulsion in his eyes.

'And you went back for more...?' he asked with hoarse incredulity.

Holly gave a small wry grin. She hadn't wanted to. Her first impression of emergency medicine had been far from favourable, but in the end she'd rather enjoyed the experience, though not the occasional physical intimidation.

'Well, I didn't actually have much choice,' she began to tell him, only he jumped in, his deep voice vibrating condemnation before she had an opportunity to explain farther.

'*No choice*! Good God, woman, you always have a choice not to stay in an abusive relationship,' he told her contemptuously. 'At sixteen I put your choice of boyfriend down to inexperience!' Even amid this bewildering tirade of condemnation, his brief allusion to their last mortifying meeting made her blush. 'But you obviously get some sort of perverted kick out of being knocked around.'

It finally dawned on a mystified Holly how he had interpreted her words. She opened her mouth to tell him just how wrong he was—it would be nice to see the smug, sanctimonious snake squirm a bit—when she stopped.

She didn't owe Niall Wesley any explanations! How *dare* the man even *think* she was some sort of victim? Willing a cool mask of composure to obliterate the wrath that was almost choking her, she smiled with serene disinterest back up at him.

'I had no idea that you were so...*straight*!' she remarked with wide-eyed wonderment.

'If by straight—' grimly, he mimicked her derisive tone '—you mean I can't abide men who consider a casual left hook an *acceptable* display of their affection, then I am just that. And if you think you can change him—forget it! Men like that don't change.' Ironically, in his present mood he looked far more daunting than any brutish drunk she'd ever had to deal with in the line of duty.

Part of Holly wanted to applaud his statement, but another part of her wanted to punish this man for having the temerity to think even for one second...!

'Why, you old softie you,' she pouted prettily up at him as she daringly placed an affectionate hand on his thigh.

Niall's lips curled with distaste as he forcibly removed her gently curling fingers as though she were contagious, but not before she had been able to note that his muscular thighs were rock hard. There was a sickening lurch in the pit of her belly.

'Don't wind me up, Holly,' he warned darkly.

Meeting the warning glimmer in his eyes, Holly felt even dizzier. 'For a gentle soul,' she told him, in a voice that emerged disastrously shaky, 'you have a firm grip.' She looked pointedly at her fingers crushed in his ruthless grasp. She despised herself for the unmistakable sensations the contact was sending through her tense body.

He released her with a selfconscious grimace. 'I'm sorry.'

'Don't worry,' she told him flexing her fingers to encourage the circulation. 'I'm yours—why, hell! I'm *anybody's*—to crush and maim.' This time she wasn't able to hide her simmering anger and he saw it too in the overbright feverish glint of her dark, spikily fringed eyes.

If she hadn't known for sure that Niall Wesley was unacquainted with the emotion, she'd have thought that there was a flicker of uncertainty in the blue eyes that skimmed over her face.

'You seem an intelligent girl...'

'Why, thank you!' she gushed insincerely. Did this man practise being patronising?

His lips thinned. 'I know you've got some sort of chip on your shoulder, Holly...'

There he goes again with this chip thing, she fumed silently. He's got me down as the original inadequate.

'...and I appreciate that Rowena must be a hard act to follow...'

As if I need it spelled out that I'm never going to be able to hold a candle to Rowena!

'But your self-esteem must be in a sorry state if you allow...' He gritted his teeth as disgust threatened to overcome him at the thought of some guy... 'You like to give the impression you're something of a free spirit, but can't you see there's nothing particularly liberating about letting some bully push you around...?'

Holly inhaled sharply and her slight but shapely bosom inflated with wrath, a circumstance which unexpectedly distracted Niall.

'Do go on,' Holly urged him bitterly.

'I don't suppose it's any of my business,' he announced with the strained air of a man who realised he'd just been speculating how far down the loose bodice of her dress would come with one judicious tug.

The very brief glimpse he'd had of her small, sweet breasts had been a tantalising, persistent presence in the back of his mind ever since he'd walked in on her. Such sensual preoccupation wouldn't have been so disturbing had the female involved not been pretty obviously screwed up, too young and the kid sister of one of his best friend's to boot! You've got plenty of problems without adding that one, he reminded himself.

'My word, but you catch on slowly.' Smiling sourly, she met his brooding stare head on. For a man so firmly against violence, he looked about ready to strangle her.

'Point taken.' His voice carried a zero level of conviction but unexpectedly he seemed to want to let the subject drop. 'We'll be there in a minute. You are going to behave?'

He looked so suspicious that she couldn't resist a naughty grin and a sing-song taunt, 'That's for me to know and you to—'

He bent forwards so suddenly that she didn't have time to protest. Mouth closed, he pressed his lips firmly to hers and kissed her hard. Firmly enough to force her head back against the seat. Holly smelt his light cologne and the warm male fragrance that drifted off his body. Her fingers and toes curled tightly as she held herself painfully rigid and inhaled deeply. Somewhere deep down she knew for sure that if she relaxed even fractionally she'd just disintegrate.

Drawing back he murmured. 'I was out of order.'

Ironically, she knew he wasn't talking about the kiss; he seemed scarcely to have noticed he'd done it. Certainly his breathing hadn't altered dramatically like her own and his skin tone wasn't making any of the dramatic fluctuations hers was. I noticed all right—boy, oh boy, did I notice!

'Your life is your own—'

'So are my lips—' A woman who was seduced by a kiss that said *shut up*, loud and clear, had serious problems.

He ignored her ironic interjection while he silently called himself all sorts of fool for giving into the stupid juvenile impulse. '…to mess up as you choose.' He held up his hands in culpability as the taxi drew up outside the hotel.

Nice touch, she thought admiringly: I'm sorry, even if you're wrong anyway. In less fraught circumstances, she might have managed a wry smile, but right at that second she didn't feel much like smiles, wry or otherwise!

If he hadn't stopped when he did…I was going to open my mouth…Wasn't!…Was!…The dizzying squabble of admission and denial was going round and round in her spinning head. The odd achy sensation deep in the pit of her stomach just wouldn't go away, any more than the distinctive male smell of him lingering in her nostrils would.

'It would be a good idea if you turned down the aggravation level.'

It would be a better idea if she flung herself from the moving vehicle! 'Is that an order?'

Without waiting for him to play the gallant—a role very much against his character—she slipped out of the taxi. Fresh air, that would do the trick she decided with more optimism than conviction. She hoped she sounded the sort of cool sophisticated female who didn't fall to pieces when an amazingly handsome male casually kissed her.

It hadn't helped her calm levels when she'd found he had been staring, rather obviously, at the silk-covered outline of her nipples which were so painfully engorged it would have taken several layers of arctic insulation, not just a bra—which she wasn't wearing—to disguise the shameful fact.

'Only if that's what you want it to be,' his voice followed her. 'Actually, it was a request. Just try to keep in mind we are meant to be deeply in love!' he added sardonically, as he paid the driver and re-joined her.

Walking into an expensive restaurant beside Niall Wesley had always been one of her more pleasurable fantasies—in retrospect, her fantasies had all been rather innocent. Dream fulfilment was a major let-down, she decided, as with a slightly mocking grin he stood to one side to let her enter the plush foyer before him. Oh, yes, he had nice manners now, after he'd ripped her character to shreds, lectured her and, to cap it all, kissed her in such a manner that left her wanting more. How she *loathed* Niall Wesley!

'You're late!' The cloud of expensive perfume reached Holly but the shapely arms didn't—they reached Niall.

Holly watched as Tara threw her arms around her ex-husband's neck and kissed him warmly on the lips. Her glossy blonde hair was long enough to reach the hand he had automatically placed around her impossibly slender waist. Just looking at the cleavage revealed by her low-cut black sheath dress made Holly feel hopelessly inadequate.

Holly averted her eyes. She didn't actually want to see if this kiss stayed as chaste as the one she'd received. One thing that had struck her before she'd looked away was that Tara Steel was indisputably more lovely in the flesh than she was on the covers of glossies!

'You've got lipstick on you, darling,' Tara clucked huskily, dabbing a tissue to the corner of Niall's mouth. He accepted her ministrations, looking at her warmly from beneath the lazy droop of his heavy-lidded eyes. 'And it's not mine.' This time there was a note of teasing disappointment mingled with the gentle reproach.

'Hello.' She looked at Holly with keen interest and then enquiringly at Niall. 'He's been so secretive, he didn't even tell me your name. In fact, I was starting to think you were a figment of his fertile imagination. I've never known a man quite as imaginative as Niall.' She shot Niall an intimate knowing look that made Holly feel quite queasy.

'And have you known many? Men that is?' The words were out before Holly could bite them back. Maybe I should let Niall do the talking, she thought.

Tara looked startled and then surprisingly she laughed. Holly wouldn't have blamed her if she'd stormed off in a huff or thrown something at her. 'Not half as many as the tabloids would have you believe...'

'Holly,' Niall supplied belatedly, in reply to Tara's questioning look. He bent forwards to pull out a chair for Holly. 'Don't worry,' he whispered in her ear. 'Jealous is good.'

Holly felt the mortified blush swallow up her normal interesting pallor. 'I didn't mean to be...rude.'

'That's a first,' Niall remarked, this time in a dry voice for everyone's ears. He took his place at the table between the two women.

'Don't tease, Niall. No, Holly, you were just reminding me that I'm yesterday's news which, under the circumstances, is fair enough.' Holly responded to the dazzling smile and candid admission with a weak smile of her own. 'You mustn't mind me, Holly. I'll always have a soft spot for this man.'

A soft spot at the very least, Holly surmised, startled by the genuine rapport that seemed to exist between the estranged couple. It might have been a trick of the light, but Holly thought she actually saw tears trembling on the end of those preposterously long lashes—they *couldn't* be real!

God, I'm a cow, Holly thought, appalled by her mean thought. How on earth could Niall not want Tara back? she wondered. Tara wasn't just incredibly sexy and lovely, she was *nice*!

'If I'd known about you earlier, I'd never have made such a fool of myself trying to rekindle the old flame. But you mustn't be jealous; from what Niall has told me he's *devoted* to you.'

On the receiving end of Niall's best devoted smile, Holly made an agonised sound in her throat. Fortunately, Tara seemed to interpret her inarticulate protest as a lover-like murmur, and she smiled benignly at the couple. Holly felt nauseous—she just wasn't equipped to deal with this sort of prolonged deception! She wanted to leap to her feet and shriek, he doesn't love me! He didn't even remember my name!

'Now I've seen you I can see why, and he tells me you love children…But then, Niall would never marry anyone who didn't. Thomas is the centre of his world and I'm so glad he finally has someone to share the responsibility. He's a marvellous father—which is just as well, as I'm such an awful mother.'

'You know that's rubbish,' Niall denied immediately, his dark, strongly delineated brows drawing together in a straight line of disapproval. 'Thomas is as proud as hell of his mother and always will be, and you can direct anyone who says different to me.'

Holly had never had a man announce he'd fight the world and his brother on her behalf. She felt decidedly surplus to requirements and, for some ridiculous reason, perilously close to tears in the midst of this mutual admiration.

Where was the vitriol, where was the tension? This matiness just wasn't normal. How could you stay friends with someone you'd once been married to? Surely the feelings of betrayal and anger couldn't just disappear overnight? She was pretty certain she couldn't be so civilised if she found herself in the same position, but they seemed to agree on everything. So why, she wondered, had they ever broken up?

Tara misted up prettily and she bit her quivering lip. 'You've been so good after all I did,' she said huskily. 'I'm so happy to see you've finally found someone of your own. It's positively mystical.' Tara's warm mellow purr dropped to a wondering whisper.

'*Mystical?*' Niall queried warily.

Holly stared. If I'd said anything with *half* as much mockery potential, he'd have ripped me to shreds with that nasty tongue of his, she thought, studying his tolerant expression with disbelief.

'It's spooky. My astrologer told me the other day that this was going to happen to one of my dearest friends—I didn't know at the time she was talking about you two.'

'Astrologer?' Holly echoed. Nice but nutty, she concluded, correcting her mental profile of the beautiful woman.

'Yes, she's incredible. I never make any major decisions without consulting her, do I, Niall?'

'Indeed you don't,' Niall confirmed drily.

'She only takes clients by recommendation, but I could introduce you if you like, Holly. She was incredibly helpful when we were splitting up…Not that I'm suggesting you two are going to…'

'No thanks,' Holly responded hastily. 'I like to think I control my own fate.'

'Oh I can see you're a sceptic like Niall.' She threw her ex-husband a tolerant smile. 'Tell me, Holly, what do you think of Thomas? Isn't he just the greatest kid?'

'I…I haven't met him yet.' Holly crossed her fingers and hoped that she wasn't contradicting anything Niall had said.

'Really?'

Holly wasn't surprised by Tara's amazement. If Niall ever did remarry it sounded to her very much like his son, closely followed by his beautiful ex-wife, would have the final say. If the child gave the thumbs-down, then it was goodbye lover! She pitied the woman who would find herself in this situation.

'How could she?' Niall put in smoothly. 'You know the boy's been staying with Chris and Jude in Maine for the past four weeks. It was you who persuaded me to let him go, remember.'

'Well, he and little Daniel get on so well, I thought it…' She stopped, an arrested expression drifting over her flawless features. 'You mean you've only known one another for a few weeks? I had the impression…Do your parents know, Niall?'

'Only you know, Tara, and we'd like it to stay that way.'

Holly shot him a look of alarm. It better had, the explanations could get embarrassing if this ever got out.

'Even though I've known Holly since she was a kid with braces, all *this* is new…' He caught one of Holly's hands between both of his and brought the tips of her fingers up to his mouth.

He had that part right, Holly reflected grimly. 'Very new,' she agreed drily, tucking the hand he'd released neatly under the table.

There was warning glitter in the blue eyes that rested on her face. 'We've hardly got used to the idea ourselves,' he told Tara frankly. 'And don't start with any horror stories about my parents. Holly is already scared stiff at the idea of meeting them, aren't you, darling?' He gazed lovingly into her eyes. The rat had missed his true vocation in life. What an actor! He recovered the hand which lay protectively in her lap and covered it with his before lifting it to softly brush the inside of her wrist against his lips.

Despite the fact that all her wary barriers were firmly in place, the soft contact sent a neat electrical current zinging through her body.

'No,' she contradicted firmly. She might be playing a part but there were limits. If he expected her to flutter her eyelashes and cling to his strong hand, he could think again! Scared, indeed! Wasn't it fear of another kind that was making her heart pound? She pushed aside this inconvenient thought.

'A little natural apprehension, possibly,' she conceded firmly, trying to inconspicuously free the hand which Niall had appropriated.

Before Holly could give her order to the hovering drinks waiter, Niall spoke up for her—she so hated it when men did that!

'Holly will have a mineral water, won't you, darling?' His malicious smile dared her to contradict him.

Holly's nostrils flared and her dark eyes were filled with contempt, but she smiled back in a suitably besotted manner. 'Whatever you say, sweetheart.' It would seem that Tara watching this tender interchange, couldn't detect sarcasm—even when it was ladled on with a trowel.

When the waiter had gone, Holly soon discovered just what the overimaginative Tara *had* been detecting from his overbearing manner and her meek submission.

'You're pregnant!' She clapped her hands. 'I should have guessed. This is marvellous,' she enthused.

Holly looked at her blankly. Great, not only do I have his ex-wife's blessing to marry him, I have her approval to reproduce, too. Is this situation off the scale of weird or is it just me?

Tara smiled warmly at Holly's stunned face. 'She's got a definite glow about her, hasn't she, Niall?'

Holly didn't know about a glow but she did feel as though she might spontaneously combust any second from pure mortification. She sent a glance of desperate appeal to Niall, who seemed to be taking this suggestion in his stride. To add insult to injury, as he looked with interest at her pink cheeks and horrified eyes, he even seemed slightly amused.

'I think Holly's radiance lights up any room she walks into, but I'm a trifle biased. Sorry to disappoint you, Tara, but she's not pregnant. There are other reasons for a person to request a soft drink.' His voice dropped a sexy octave as he continued huskily, 'And other reasons for a person to get married, too.' At the last moment, he turned his riveting eyes, filled with lots of reasons—all erotic—directly towards Holly, reducing her to a frozen state of open-mouthed bemusement.

She bit her lower lip in an effort to tear her glance away from that callous, calculating seduction. She didn't doubt for a second that he expected her, like every other female, to be reduced to a gibbering idiot. He knew all right about the power his blue eyes had over the opposite sex.

'No…' She cleared her throat and turned her attention to Tara. 'He thinks I've got a drink problem,' she confided with a gusty sigh.

Tara obviously didn't know whether to take Holly's

words seriously or not. Uncertainly, she looked from Holly to a frozen-faced Niall and back again.

'You're joking…Right?'

'Yes Tara, she's joking.' Finally, she'd pierced his sardonic cool. 'Holly has a *very* warped sense of humour.'

Holly heard the controlled warning in his voice and stifled a grin. 'I thought, *darling*—' she raised her eyes guilelessly to his '—that you loved everything about me.'

At that moment, the waiter enquired if they were ready to give their order.

'You order for me, darling.' Holly produced her best helpless little woman look and received a murderous glare for her troubles. 'I'm so hopeless at that sort of thing.'

'Don't squabble!' Tara pleaded. 'I can see you two enjoy it, but I just *hate* it!'

Holly shot the older woman a startled glance. They were enjoying it? Where did she get that crazy idea? She looked sideways and discovered that Niall was looking at her with an expression that suggested he was just as startled as she was by this preposterous notion.

'Tell me, Holly, what do you do?'

'Drives me to distraction, mostly,' Niall forestalled her reply.

Obviously, she brooded darkly, he had concluded that whatever she did for a living wouldn't be good enough for the prospective wife of a powerful and influential figure like himself. As it happened, a junior doctor who didn't have a minute to call her own probably was about as unsuitable as you could get.

'Did I mention that Holly is Rowena Parish's sister?'

'Really, I'd never have guessed! You know, Niall,' Tara mused thoughtfully, 'I thought that if you ever married again it would be Rowena. Actually, Holly,' she added in a wry aside, 'when we were first married I was rather jealous of your sister and all their blood-brother pals act. If you know what I mean.'

Holly, who could identify completely with this comment, nodded.

'It's ironic, isn't it?' Tara laughed.

'You never told me that!' Niall exclaimed in a shocked voice. There was a dark band of colour across the slanting sweep of his high cheekbones.

Guilty conscience? Holly wondered uncharitably. Well, she couldn't see a single reason why she should give Niall the benefit of the doubt.

'Well, I wouldn't, would I, silly.'

The loud sound of a chair being pushed over made them and every other diner in the restaurant turn around.

'Oh, help, please, someone!' An attractive woman was down on her knees beside the figure of a prone middle-aged man. 'I don't think he's breathing!' she wailed.

Holly wasn't very far behind Niall as he moved towards the traumatised woman. He was feeling the man's neck for a pulse when she dropped down on her knees.

'Nothing,' he said shaking his head. He started to loosen the tie around the portly man's neck and the anxious companion began to wail in earnest, throwing herself bodily on top of the man.

'Let me…' Holly began.

'Will you look after the woman?' Niall curtly cut her off. 'Has someone called an ambulance?'

'I have, sir,' the *maître d'* confirmed, materialising at their side. He took the distraught woman by the arm and pulled her to one side. He looked on doubtfully as Niall struck the man sharply on the chest and tilted his head back in readiness to begin mouth-to-mouth. 'Don't you think, sir, we should wait until a doctor arrives?'

CHAPTER THREE

'I AM a doctor,' Holly said, sparing him a brief glance before she began chest compressions. 'One, two...' She began to count out loud.

Briefly her eyes met Niall's. 'Game, set and match, you witch,' he conceded.

'Save your breath,' Holly advised. 'He needs it.'

The man had, much to her relief, started breathing before the paramedics had arrived. Holly was glad to see a familiar face. She gave a brief concise history to the big hunky paramedic, who listened and nodded as he gave the patient a quick assessment.

'Just can't keep away from me, can you, Doc Parish?' He winked broadly at her. 'Nice one,' he added approvingly, nodding toward the figure on the stretcher. 'We'll take over now.'

'Thank you, Paul.'

'No, thank you, my sweet.' He smiled warmly over his shoulder as they whisked the man off to the waiting ambulance. 'We miss you already, Holly!'

Niall had watched this interchange through narrowed eyes and wondered if he looked as much of a fool as he felt—probably not. He felt *extremely* foolish!

'Why didn't you tell me?' he demanded.

Holly inclined her head up towards the tall, grim-faced figure beside her. 'Why didn't you ask?'

Several people called out congratulatory comments as

she made her way back to the table, where a shaken-looking Tara was drinking a large brandy. Tara got to her feet and enfolded Holly in a warm fragrant embrace.

'You were so marvellous! Wasn't she, Niall? I don't know how you stayed so calm. I'm shaking like a leaf.' She released Holly and held out a hand to demonstrate. 'Well, now I know what you do.'

Holly, whose nails were kept conveniently short, envied the beautifully polished perfect set of nails the other woman had.

'I shake, too—inside, at least.'

'It must be marvellous knowing you can help people.'

'It's lucky she doesn't live in a litigious country where she has to think twice about helping someone,' Niall contributed wryly.

Thinking of Tara's breathless sentiments, Holly nodded a little selfconsciously. With her friends and colleagues, she might have responded with a facetious remark which would have had them all laughing. Perhaps one day she'd develop the veneer of cynicism that many of her colleagues had, but deep down she agreed with Tara: she was lucky to be doing something she enjoyed so much.

'It's also extremely tiring,' she responded lightly. 'The hours are not exactly conducive to a social life either.'

'I can imagine,' Tara, who knew all about long gruelling hours, agreed.

Holly's eyes twinkled as she gave a naughty smile. 'But there are fringe benefits. Did you notice him...?' she asked, her tongue firmly inserted in her cheek.

'He was hard to miss,' Tara responded immediately. 'There's something about a man in uniform...' she mused with a twinkle.

'Isn't there just,' Holly agreed with lascivious fervour.

'Shall I leave?' Despite his languid tone, Holly had the

impression Niall wasn't over the moon about their conversation.

'Don't tell me a bit of girlie talk is making you of all people feel insecure, Niall?' Tara teased.

'I wouldn't like to be responsible for cramping your style, ladies.'

'You won't,' Holly promised with a sweetly malicious smile.

'Seriously, Holly, I know it's hard to juggle a career and a marriage, but with a supportive partner anything's possible.' Tara, sitting beside her ex-partner, seemed genuinely unaware of any irony in her statement.

'There aren't many partners *that* supportive,' Holly responded cynically. She'd seen marriages stretched to the limit break under the strain.

'Well, you don't have to look, do you? Because you've found one.' She looked across the table at Niall and smiled warmly. 'You know I'm so glad he's marrying you and not Rowena. I'm sure she's a very nice person,' she added anxiously as Holly shot her a quizzical look. 'But you two look sort of right together. And just look how well you worked together just now.'

There hadn't been time to wonder during the panic, but now a disturbed and squirming Holly could recall how, bizzarely, Niall had seemed to know what she wanted him to do before she asked him when they had worked in unison to save the man's life. If he anticipated a woman's—or, more specifically, *her*—needs that well in other, more pleasurable, situations, it would be quite something, she reflected.

For several dreamy seconds, she let her mind dwell speculatively on the steamy sensual images that floated into her head.

'Sure, we're soul mates from way back.'

The blistering sarcasm in his voice made Tara look at him with shocked disapproval and woke Holly from the erotic permutations she'd been spinning around the general bedroom theme. Her eyes opened wide with dismay as a horrified fractured sigh emerged from her dry lips.

'You're tired,' Niall observed, noticing her sigh, but fortunately not knowing the cause.

He sounded concerned, if a little cross, as though she'd got tired just to irritate him, but the tender lover was all part of the act, she reminded herself, burying her nose in a balloon of brandy that Tara had pushed into her hands to avoid looking directly at him.

All this talk of supportive, understanding partners was making her feel all soft and sentimental, not to mention just a mite wistful. Then she'd made the criminally stupid mistake of imagining what sort of lover Niall would make.

Pretending that she didn't find him wildly attractive wasn't going to get her anywhere, she told herself with stern pragmatism. What she had to do was keep her imagination on a strict rein. She was grown up; she didn't have to go broadcasting the fact she was privately lusting after his body. And it is just his body, it's that superficial, she told herself firmly. I don't even *like* the man, for goodness' sake!

She knew there were a lot of women in Niall Wesley's life and, even if he had displayed any interest in her, Holly had no wish to join the ranks of his mistresses. There seemed to be two very important women his life—Niall's beautiful ex-wife and her own sister. A wise woman knew when not to compete. No, her relationship with Niall was going to stay safely in the realms of make-believe!

Holly was relieved when Niall made their excuses early. Sitting in the taxi on the journey home, he didn't seem inclined to talk. When he did, the sound of his deep voice made her jump.

'I suppose a boyfriend didn't give you the black eye, either?' There was resigned certainty in his voice. 'In the line of duty…?'

Holly nodded and continued to pretend a great interest in the traffic that was crawling past in the next lane. 'A drunk with a head wound got a bit out of hand. Actually, it was Paul, the paramedic you saw earlier, who pulled him off.'

'A versatile guy.' For a muscle-bound freak.

'He's a very nice person.' It was bad enough to be on the receiving end of Niall's sneers without having her friends coming in for the same treatment.

'Don't they have any sort of security in these places?' Niall wondered disapprovingly.

'Of course they have security.'

'It just doesn't work very well.'

Her shoulders lifted in concession. 'Not always.'

'Why did you let me drone on and on?'

'Because you seem to like the sound of your own voice…' With a rueful little smile she broke off and, clasping both her palms together, rested her lips against the peak of her fingertips. 'Actually, I was mad as hell because you'd thought I could be the sort of woman who would tolerate an abusive relationship. You were being intolerably patronising, condescending and sanctimonious.'

'Don't hold back, will you? Tell me exactly how you feel.'

Niall, who had been on the receiving end of many a smile of practised seduction, found her small lop-sided little grin had a curious charm.

'I can see your point.'

'You can?' Startled, she looked directly at him for the first time since this conversation had begun.

'You seemed to get on with Tara—very well.'

'I liked her.' But not as much as you do! She gave a tight smile. 'I didn't like deceiving her.'

'Don't worry, it was all in a good cause. Tara in self-sacrifice mode is hard to stop.'

'How are you going to explain it to her when you don't get married?'

'Don't worry about my imagination; it hasn't let me down yet.'

'Tara said as much,' she grunted.

Niall's dark brows shot upwards and Holly blushed in case he realised she'd spent more time than she ought to thinking about the implications of this statement.

'I take it your Sleeping Beauty act wasn't the result of prolonged debauchery, either?'

'It was a mistake to go for a farewell drink after a very long and busy weekend on call, especially as the drink turned into an impromptu party. Oh, God!' she yelped suddenly clamping a hand to her forehead.

'What's wrong?'

'I haven't called Mum.' And then she added, in case he thought it odd that a woman of her age felt obliged to contact her parents at regular intervals, 'she'll be imagining me in some dreadful scrape.'

This overprotective maternal concern was all because she'd been a little bit accident-prone as a child. When she'd tried to tell her mother she didn't go around climbing trees any more, her parent had said in her best I-know-better-than-you voice, 'Worse things than falling out of trees happen to big girls.' Holly's youthful insistence that she was a *big girl now* was a standing joke in their family because, as it turned out, she never had got big.

Her dark eyes sparkled with sudden mischievous mockery. 'I can always get on my broomstick if the line's busy.'

Niall found the mercurial shift of her expression strangely compelling. He couldn't remember the last time he'd felt this much interest in a woman.

'I didn't say I have anything against witches...Especially if they have auburn hair, an exceptional body and skin like milk.' He tilted his head to one side and let his gleaming eyes dwell lingeringly on the attributes he'd just so lovingly described.

Holly listened with a detached sense of disbelief to his husky drawl. My God, is he making a pass at me? Niall Wesley making a pass! It struck her with painful clarity that dream scenarios were a very inadequate preparation for reality. She discovered that although her whole body was aching with a very undreamlike need, she was repelled by the idea he was just going through the motions, the same way he probably did any time he found himself in a promising situation with a woman.

'The orthodontist did a good job on my teeth, too. Do you want to take a look?' she snapped, furious with him for being so superficially obvious. 'Flirting wasn't in the script,' she reminded him gruffly. If he had an ounce of sensitivity, they might be able to avoid an embarrassing scene.

'I'm improvising.' In direct defiance of the small voice of sanity in the back of his skull, the one that said this wasn't the sort of girl he wanted to get involved with. She was cranky, plagued by insecurities and had a viperous tongue.

It didn't escape her notice that he hadn't denied the flirting part—so she wasn't imagining things—not that the sizzling sensuality in his eyes left much room for doubt. Holly clenched her fists into tight balls and her gusty breath made the soft copper tendrils around her face gently dance.

'Then start!' she demanded fiercely.

'You seem insulted.' He didn't consider himself a particularly vain man, but her response wasn't exactly flattering. She was definitely attracted to him, too; he hadn't passed thirty without being able to pick up on these things.

'Is there someone else?'

She shook her head. 'If you're worried I'll be insulted if you don't ask, don't. I won't be. I don't think your reputation as a superstud will suffer too much if you take one night off.' Chewing her full lower lip, she tugged off the ring and thrust it out to him without meeting his eyes.

The last little flicker of humour left his face. Niall couldn't recall the last time he'd felt this frustrated by a woman. What was it about about this red-headed witch, who seemed completely unaware she'd insulted him by implying he was promiscuous? he brooded darkly. Did she think he had actively courted the reputation the media had lumbered him with? Did she think he enjoyed it?

'Actually,' he said, receiving the ring with a curt inclination of his head, 'I don't make love to *everyone* I share a cab with...only the females,' he added with blighting sarcasm.

Holly was aware she'd made him angry and tried to retrieve the situation. 'You know what I mean. I'm not saying there's anything wrong with your attitude to sex,' she told him kindly.

'That's very open-minded of you.'

Had she bruised his ego? He was certainly looking at her a bit oddly. 'Perhaps I'm just not a very spontaneous person.' She didn't care if she sounded terminally prim. 'I probably take more time deciding which breakfast cereal to buy than you do choosing your partners.'

Niall's nostrils quivered. 'I can remember a time when you asked me to teach you how to kiss—that seemed pretty spontaneous,' he taunted, ripping impatiently at the knot of his constricting tie.

It took Holly several seconds to collect her startled wits. 'A cheap shot,' she told him with reproachful candour. 'I don't know what you hope to achieve by dredging that up!'

Niall's colour deepened. He wasn't sure, either. As he recalled, the occasion had been the perfect ending to the weekend from hell, which had started with the discovery that the man who had got his kid sister pregnant was married!

'I was way out of line, not to mention seeing the world through cider-tinted spectacles,' she admitted, uncomfortable at the memory. 'But I was a kid, you weren't, and you were far tougher on me than the situation warranted. In fact,' she told him frankly, 'you were fairly vicious.'

It wasn't as if she'd had any street cred to lose when she'd drunk the first glass of cider at a private park, she had just naively assumed that cider was a fairly innocuous drink. Even though she'd got tipsy, things would have been all right if her parents had been waiting up for her as they usually did, but the house had been in darkness when she'd arrived home.

Feeling like a sophisticated woman of the world, Holly had offered to make her escort a coffee. The sophisticated feeling had lasted until they got as far as the sitting room and he'd pounced. What could only be termed an undignified struggle ensued and Holly panicked.

The struggle had come to an abrupt halt when a table lamp had been switched on. The fight had magically gone right out of her would-be seducer when Niall emerged sleepy-eyed, bare-chested and very irritably from his makeshift bed on the sofa. When he'd actually got to his feet, the boy had taken one look at Niall, all six foot plus of perfectly muscled manhood, and without a word had fled.

Holly had hardly noticed him go. She'd never been this close to an almost naked man before and it, or maybe the cider, was making her feel quite odd. She hadn't known that men could be that beautiful, but Niall was.

He had sounded quite concerned when he asked her if she was all right. Holly had nodded mutely and tried to straighten her dishevelled clothes and mussed-up hair. Then, looking stern but kindly, Niall had begun to say a lot of things to her that her father already had. It was one thing to be read a lecture by her dad, quite another to be censured by the man of her youthful dreams! Holly had burned with humiliation—he was talking to her as if she were a kid.

'Besides,' Niall had said, coming to a light-hearted conclusion, 'It was no loss. The groper didn't look like he could kiss. I should wait until you find someone who—'

The condescension on top of her humiliation was just too much to take. Hands on her narrow hips, chin and chest thrust aggressively out, she blurted, 'If you're so good at it, why don't *you* teach me how to kiss?'

Niall had looked at her in a way that made her feel about two inches tall and slightly grubby, to boot! That's when he'd *really* laid into her, annihilating her character in blisteringly forthright terms.

Niall cleared his throat and looked, much to her amazement, self-consciously uncomfortable. If she hadn't known he didn't suffer from self-doubt, she might have suspected he had doubts himself about how he'd handled the situation he'd found himself thrust into. A situation which, she readily acknowledged, most young men would have found horrific.

'It's sometimes kinder to be cruel, and I'd call that kick you landed pretty vicious.' Better to be accused of going over the top than not noticing a potentially dangerous situation that was staring him in the face. His expression grew bleak as his thoughts turned to his sister Jude.

'It was a lucky shot,' she told him, recalling how scared she'd been when, on the one and only time in her life she'd ever resorted to physical violence, the big strong man had sunk, winded and in obvious agony, to his knees. 'And it wasn't just cruel to call me a stupid little tart,' she pointed out acidly, 'it was untrue. I just hope for your son's sake your ideas of enlightened child guidance have mellowed over the years.'

Niall's angular jaw tightened at this scathing reference to his parenting skills. 'I take it you've been harbouring a grudge all these years,' he deduced with incredulous scorn. 'It really has made your day, having the opportunity to knock me back. Or is the rejection meant to pique my interest?'

'Your humility makes me feel humble. There's a much simpler and more likely explanation, but I can see that's too revolutionary so I'll spell it out. I just don't fancy you, Niall.'

He raised one irritatingly sceptical brow and repressed an uncivilised urge to make her eat her words. It would be a pleasure, he thought, examining the lush contours of her wilful mouth.

'Your mouth's saying one thing; those big hungry eyes are saying something quite different.'

The *smug*…The problem was, he was right. Her slender back felt exposed as a prickle of fear ran the length of her stiff spine. No matter how much she denied it, she knew she was sexually aware of Niall as a rampantly attractive male with every fibre of her hot sticky body. Holly hoped and prayed that all he could see in her eyes right now was sarcastic contempt. She wiped the palms of her sweaty hands nervously against her thighs.

'If it makes you and your ego happier to think that, that's fine by me.'

Niall laughed, there was arrogant confidence in the sound. Cheeks flaming, teeth grating, Holly decided to maintain a dignified but frigid silence for the rest of the journey.

He didn't walk her into the building; she didn't care about that, but after saving his skin you'd have thought he would have the common courtesy to thank her. Why am I surprised? she asked herself. He's nothing but a rich spoilt playboy and Rowena and Tara are welcome to him!

CHAPTER FOUR

'YOU'RE staying for the weekend when you pick up Thomas.' There was no hint of doubt in the confident voice on the other end of the line.

Niall sighed and gave a thumbs-up sign to his assistant, who was still awaiting his response to a question. The door closed behind the quietly efficient individual.

'I *suppose* I could,' he confirmed reluctantly. Giving his diary a quick mental review, he felt a stab of affectionate irritation. He was used to his mother's interference but this didn't alter the fact he hated being organised, and she knew it.

This was the longest time he'd ever spent without his son. He'd been eagerly looking forward to having Tom to himself when the boy got back from his Stateside holiday. Looking at it objectively—something he rarely did, where his son was concerned—he supposed that he was being selfish. His parents didn't see as much of the boy as they liked.

'And bring her with you.'

Niall stopped twirling the pen between his fingers. 'Her who...?' he enquired ungrammatically.

'Her, your fiancée,' came back the smooth response.

Niall dropped the pen on the floor. He hadn't calculated for Tara talking to his mother—he ought to have! Silently he cursed himself for not noticing this giant flaw in his otherwise excellent plan.

'What are you talking about, Mother?'

His bored tone didn't have the desired effect on his mother—but it had been worth a try.

'Don't waste all that on me. I've been speaking to Tara. Really, Niall, if you want to keep a secret, she is the very worst person to confide in. She tells me this girl is very nice—but, as Tara could see some good in a mass murderer, I'm reserving judgement. As for all this nonsense about getting used to the situation!' A scornful sound of disgust reached ears. 'Since when did you get so precious?' she demanded brusquely of her eldest born. 'What's wrong with the girl?'

'I'm not sure if Holly can make it, Mother...'

'I'm sure you can persuade her. I'm always hearing how persuasive women find you.'

Niall, who was used to his mother's bracing sarcasm remained cheerfully unstressed by the savage witticism. His mother was always very forthright when it came to commenting on his character—though only, as she often said herself, in a *constructive* way.

'I can't make any promises...'

'Nothing new there, then. You're the most evasive man I've ever come across,' Maeve Wesley continued as if he hadn't spoken. 'You know your father and I are going back with Chris and Jude to stay for a month, so it has to be this weekend. Unless you'd prefer me to come up to town to meet her? Is she living with you?'

'We'll see you this weekend, Mother.' Some things in life were inevitable, he reflected philosophically. He put the phone down and immediately redialled. What time would it be in New York, right now?

Holly looped the dangling strap of her small backpack up over one shoulder and pulled down the rucked sleeve of her short denim jacket. She frowned at the dusty mark on the toe of one of her newly acquired ankle-length boots, and surreptitiously rubbed the mark against the curve of her shapely calf, covered at this moment by the ankle-length skirt she wore. While she was still slightly off balance, someone waved something large and glittery under her nose. The same ever so slightly tip-tilted nose twitched as it immediately recognised the very faint, very exclusive fragrance.

She lost the thread of the thought that had been debating the awkward choice between linguine and tagliatelle as her heart went from quiet amble to breathless sprint in the space of a single beat. The sensation of a fist tightening in her stomach was so powerful she almost doubled over to nurse the acute pain. She made no immediate effort to make contact with those mesmeric blue eyes; instead, she took several steadying breaths first and felt deeply disgusted with herself for this feeble display of lust.

'What's this?' Holly knew perfectly well what it was. It was a ring, a sapphire ring, and she'd seen it before. She passed a hand swiftly over her mouth, blotting the light sheen of moisture along her upper lip. The skinny-rib top she wore clung damply to her spine.

At least she hadn't said, 'Who are you?' Or possibly, Niall mused, examining the hostile light in the dark brown eyes fixed on his face, starting from scratch might have been more promising. Still, he'd been prepared for this reaction. Niall prided himself that he was prepared for most things. Or maybe not…He hadn't been entirely prepared for the strength of the sexual tension that was buzzing around them.

His eyes did a distracted once over—she was really tiny, with a bone structure to match her height. He was sure he could span that waist with his hands and still have plenty of room over. In that bohemian get-up, if he hadn't known what an edible body dwelt beneath the layered look…Only, he did know. He didn't frequent supermarkets much himself but he suspected that copulation in the aisles was pretty much frowned on. *Pity.*

'And what are you doing here?' Her throat was bone dry.

'Shopping?' Niall suggested, looking intelligently at the neatly stacked shelves around them.

Holly's sceptical gaze moved from her own laden trolley to his empty hands. 'Let me give you a tip: they like you to carry a basket. Even now the store detective's probably got you under surveillance as a suspicious character.'

Actually, in his beautifully cut designer suit, he was drawing a lot of attention—and all of it, predictably, was female.

She didn't blame her fellow shoppers for goggling. Men like Niall didn't often buy baked beans in supermarkets— they didn't do anything so mundane! They were the sort of men you saw brooding dangerously in moodily lit black-and-white-ads for designer items. He was the rogue male stallion who'd strolled unexpectedly into the midst of a domestic herd, and his presence was creating a murmur of excitement—a loud murmur! She rolled her eyes, despising the fanciful analogy even as it popped into her head.

'I hoped I'd bump into you.' Words to gladden the heart of any lonely single shopper had they, unlike herself, not known what a snake in the grass he was.

'*Hoped?* I got the distinct impression you couldn't wait to see the back of me.'

'That was my frustration speaking.' Holly glared back with glacial indifference. 'All right,' he conceded, boosting the charm level of his winning smile by several hundred volts. '*Planned.* You were leaving the flat when I arrived, so I followed you.'

'I've never been stalked before. I don't think I like it.'

What the hell was he doing here? Her brain was working its way through a list of probabilities, which all on second examination proved unlikely.

Well, be realistic, Holly, he's not about to tell you that not seeing your face is keeping him awake at nights! Although she was beside herself with curiosity, she'd have died before she'd admit this shameful fact to him.

'I need your help.'

If her indiscriminate hormones didn't transform her brain into mush every time she saw him, she'd already have worked this out for herself.

'*No!*' She turned her back on him and started to pile tins into her trolley.

The large hand on her shoulder was light, but it completely immobilised Holly. 'You don't know what I'm going to say.'

'I don't need to,' she retorted. 'The answer is still *no*!'

Niall could tell she had really enjoyed saying that. Never had he heard one syllable contain so much relish. He waited a moment before spoiling her pleasure.

'Do you actually have a cat?'

Holly looked at the large pile of tins in her trolley. 'No, not yet. I like to be prepared,' she added weakly.

He didn't ridicule this ludicrous explanation, so he must really be desperate, she reflected thoughtfully. Some vague notion of holding Niall Wesley's fate in her hands flashed through her head—it was a nice, warm, comforting thought. Would he beg? She looked at his dark saturnine features and decided regretfully that this was doubtful; the man didn't have a humble bone in his beautiful body.

'We have cats at home.'

By 'home', she assumed he was talking about the ancestral pile, not his town house. 'Nice for you.'

'I'm sure you'd like them.'

Holly had had enough of his graceful dancing around the issue. 'Will you just get to the point? I've not got all day.'

'I need you to pretend to be my fiancée again…just for the weekend, this time. Tara's been talking to my mother and she told her about you. The upshot of which is, they've invited us down for the weekend. My parents are going away next month. When they come back, we can have split up and by then Tara will have gone back to her man and it won't matter.'

Not matter—oh, no, messing around with her life counted as zero in his list of priorities. Holly folded her arms and looked up at him incredulously. 'You can't imagine even for one second I'm going to agree to this.'

'Not for me, no.'

'What do you mean?' she snapped. *Not for me?*

'I was speaking to Rowena earlier. I explained the situation…She thought it was a hoot.'

Holly could almost hear her sister's musical laughter. 'And I thought I was the one with the warped sense of humour.'

'She said she was *sure* you'd be delighted to help out one of her best friends.' He smiled as those big brown eyes staring up at him gradually filled with horror. 'Let me see,' he mused, tapping his forefinger against the bridge of his masterful nose. 'The words "one favour deserves another" did come up at some point. Oh, I almost forgot. Rowena made me promise to ask you if you're enjoying staying at the flat—rent free?'

Now he made her sound like a freeloader, when in actual fact she'd wanted to pay her way. It was her magnanimous big sister who'd insisted that Holly was doing her a favour by flat-sitting.

'Are you telling me,' Holly choked, her voice shaking with outrage, 'that Rowena will throw me out of the flat if I don't help you?'

'I can't see Rowena doing that, can you?' he remonstrated gently. 'No, Rowena might be *hurt* if you didn't do a little favour for her friend, that's all. There's no obligation. She might be disappointed...' he forecast tentatively.

No obligation—oh, no, *not much*! Her temper blazed into full flagrant life. 'You're a dirty, blackmailing rat!' Her dark eyes sparkled with contempt. How she'd love to slap that smug smirk off his face! Her glare widened to encompass the girl at the delicatessen counter, who had giggled when Holly had given her rather loud assessment of his character.

'Rowena felt sure you'd do the right thing. She tells me you're very big on principles, personal honour and so forth.' He made it sound amusingly quaint.

'Much you'd know about it!' she roared contemptuously, going extremely red in the face. 'And how dare you discuss me with my sister?'

His slow provocative smile deepened. 'Scared I know all your deep dark secrets?' he taunted softly.

Holly shook her head and her short fat plait whipped around and caught her in the mouth. 'I don't have any dark secrets.'

He shook his head sympathetically. 'Rowena said as much.'

Holly took a hopeless wrathful breath. When she saw her sister...! He had her trapped. He knew she wouldn't let Rowena down; half the expensive medical books she possessed had been purchased courtesy of her big sister's generosity. Their parents weren't well off and Rowena's financial help had made life much easier in Holly's student days.

She gripped the handle of her trolley with both hands until her knuckles turned white.

'When do you want me?' she enquired with gloomy resignation. His dark brows shot up and she winced. 'Don't worry,' she told him with icy dignity. 'That wasn't an offer.'

A slow, scary grin slashed his lean dark features. 'Pity.'

Holly's lips tightened as a sensual shiver slid down her spine. Was that supposed to keep alive her furtive fantasies for the duration? Actually, her furtive fantasies were surviving without any help!

'Save the theatricals for our audience and don't blame me if they smell a rat in the first five minutes.' Her expression made it clear that the rat she was talking about stood six feet four in his bare feet!

'We'll just have to convince them, won't we, Holly?' He looked thoughtful. 'Do you think we should have pet names for one another? To give some depth to this thing?'

'What did you have in mind?' She could think of one or two things she'd like to call him!

'How about "poppet"? You look a poppet sort of girl to me.'

Holly gave a very unpoppet-like growl. 'If you want to live, don't ever call me that!' she told him with deep sincerity.

Niall's lips quivered. 'Anything you say,' he promised, as she strode off at a rattling pace guaranteed not to leave a single egg so meticulously ticked off her grocery list intact.

*   *   *

'So your sister married an American and they live in Maine.' Her brain was spinning from the information he'd been force-feeding her on the journey out of the city.

'No, they live in New York. They have a summer house in Maine, which is where Thomas has been staying. They have a son a couple of years older than Tom, as well as a new baby. I've warned Mother that we want to break the news of our marriage to Tom in our own time, and as far as Tom's concerned she'll respect my wishes.' He only wished this respect extended into other aspects of his life. 'So there's no worries there.'

When he talked this way, it felt almost as if the whole thing was real. Holly had caught herself at some points during the last hour, while she'd been memorising family details, feeling as if all this was for real and she actually was going to meet her future in-laws. Fortunately, the rational part of her brain kept her feet firmly rooted in reality.

'It's unusual, isn't it?'

'What's unusual?' He didn't take his eyes off the monotony of the motorway. As was to be expected, Niall was a good driver; though, rather to her surprise, no speed-fiend.

'It's not usual for the child to live with his father.' And the way she recalled it from newspaper stories Thomas had only been a baby when his parents split up. 'And you're not the most obvious—'

'Nurturing figure?' he suggested drily as, deciding she might have said too much, her rambling observations abruptly ceased—but not for long.

'But how could Tara—' she began thoughtlessly.

'Desert her child?' he bit out. The deep-set eyes that skimmed over her face held an arctic chill. 'She didn't. Tara sees Tom whenever she can. He stays with her when it's reasonable for him to do so.'

Which couldn't be often, considering Tara's globe-trotting lifestyle. Glancing at Niall's set profile, she kept this observation to herself.

'She loves him,' he continued, 'but he lives with me.'

'I wasn't criticising.'

'Yes, you were, and you're not saying anything that Tara hasn't heard, had said to her face, behind her back or seen in print a thousand times before. She's heard every sanctimonious permutation on the ''unnatural woman who deserted her child'' line.' A stark silence followed his grim words. 'You've no idea…'

'No, I haven't, but if everyone else there this weekend does, isn't there a strong possibility I might put my foot in it?' Her ignorance could well be the downfall of his little scheme.

A shaft of amusement lightened his expression momentarily. 'From what I've seen of you it's highly likely you'll put *both* feet in it, but,' he conceded reluctantly, 'I can see your point. History lesson: Tara comes from a big family—ten kids; she was the eldest. They were poor, absent father, her mother retreated from the grim reality of her life with the assistance of anti-depressants which, at that time, doctors like yourself handed out like sweets.'

Holly saw the inference in his eyes that she was somehow responsible for the inadequacies of the medical profession twenty years ago. She didn't interrupt, though; he was warming to his theme and she was fascinated by the picture his bleak words were drawing.

'When she should have been playing with her dolls, Tara was bringing up her brothers and sisters, something she did until her big break came. Tara has already done the parent thing,' he explained. 'She tried with Tom, but she was deeply unhappy; she felt trapped. Perhaps it would have been easier if she'd still been in love with me—but she wasn't. You know almost as much as my family now—if not more,' he added drily. 'Satisfied?'

The most obvious thing that emerged from his words was Niall's strong sense of protectiveness towards his ex-wife.

'Did you have Thomas in an effort to patch up your marriage?' Holly knew as soon as the words passed her lips that she shouldn't have voiced her thoughts out loud. Despite this, there was no need for him to look at her as though she'd suggested he was a mass murderer! It was a perfectly legitimate suspicion, considering he'd already said their marriage had been over and she personally knew a couple who had used a baby as a sort of marital band-aid.

'That's an angle that even the tabloids didn't latch on to. It would seem that medicine's gain is gutter journalism's loss.'

Holly winced. She knew this was a major insult, coming as it did from someone who had been savaged by the press. First they'd labelled him as an unpatriotic quitter for leaving the race circuit when he had the driver's number one place in the bag—'Has The Blue-Eyed Boy Lost His Nerve?' the headlines had screamed. Today's villain was tomorrow's hero; later, he'd been the loyal husband and father left holding the baby by his flighty heartless spouse, such was the fickleness and casual cruelty of the media.

'As you're so curious about the circumstances surrounding Tom's conception, I'll tell you.' Without a word, he pulled the car off the quiet country road they'd just joined and turned off the engine,

'There's really no need,' she blustered anxiously.

Niall ignored her words completely and, showing no consideration for her discomfiture, placed his hand on her chin to jerk her around to face him.

Curiosity might be a natural human reaction, but Niall wasn't feeling in an understanding mood. Her words, whether malicious or just plain clumsily misjudged, had managed to revive a host of memories that he would have preferred to forget. The worry resurfaced that somehow these old stories would one day rear their ugly heads and hurt Tom. He looked at the flustered face of his passenger without compassion. People who blundered in places they had no right to be should expect to hear a few things they might not like.

'Tom was conceived with no forward planning, and *much* pleasure.' He paused to let that sink in and watched the embarrassed colour flare in her cheeks. 'This occurred during our last attempt to make a go of things, and *yes*, he is mine, and *no*, I haven't demanded DNA testing! Does that satisfy your prurient interest?' His blue eyes raked her face contemptuously and the derision in his voice made her squirm uncomfortably in her deeply upholstered leather seat.

Even in the midst of her mortification, her imagination insisted on providing painful pictures that went with the event. And it's pretty obvious why I feel sick to my stomach, isn't it? she thought. It's never going to happen, but I can't stop imagining myself in similar sweaty situations with this man. She'd never felt such a victim to her irresponsible hormones in her life than at that moment.

The feeling of helplessness made her glare aggressively at him and pull her chin angrily from his grasp.

'Don't get mad with me because your wife prefers someone else.' Pursing her lips she pushed a rich red curl which was making an escape bid from a heavy Celtic-designed barrette that held her rebellious hair back from her face. 'I'm not about to be your whipping boy.'

Boy? he watched narrow eyed as she licked, a bit nervously perhaps the last of the pale pinkish lipstick off her full lips. The natural shade underneath was actually much more attractive. No, despite the extreme slenderness, there was nothing even *remotely* boyish about this young woman. There was a lot that was annoying, provocative and plain irritating.

Niall felt very provoked. He also felt a quite unreasonable urge to kiss those slightly parted softly pink lips—and that was her fault, too! Fortunately for her, he wasn't a man who blindly followed every base instinct.

'It's easy to see what you saw in Tara.' Though it seemed his admiration and probably a whole lot more too was alive and well in the present tense. 'It's very much more difficult to see what she ever saw in you.'

The haughty little toss of her bright head made Niall forget he was rising above his baser instincts.

At first, the kiss was as angry as his eyes; and then, as he burrowed deeper into the warm moist sweetness of her mouth and with a small lost whimper Holly wrapped her arms tight around his neck, it became something more complex and dangerous.

Holly wasn't thinking danger—she wasn't thinking at all—she was *feeling*! Her senses were bursting with the heady cocktail of stimulants bombarding her brain. The fractured moan in her throat deepened raggedly as her fingers pressed deep into the springy lushness of his ebony hair. Crazily, even the shape of his skull thrilled her all the way down to her toes.

His lips were on her neck, her eyelids…everywhere. His clever hands moved continuously, tracing the shape of every aspect of her face. The intimacy of his exploration was simply devastating. One big hand moved to the base of her spine and, fingers splayed over the small hollow at the base of her slender back, he dragged her pliant body hard against him. She gave a startled gasp as the liquid heat low in her belly became white-hot. Desire ripped away the last shreds of her restraint.

Holly wriggled sinuously and her small breasts bounced along enthusiastically before they were firmly compressed in an entirely satisfactory manner against his broad chest. The abrasive pressure against her sensitised nipples was delicious. The heavy throb of their individual pulses became intermingled and inseparable to her sensitive ears.

He wasn't still angry—this was no longer a punishment kiss—but he was hungry, demanding and aroused. This was raw sex like she'd never known it—like she'd never in her wildest dreams imagined existed! A heavy throbbing stupor invaded her limbs; it made her feverish caresses clumsy.

The first motorcycle that went past hooted its horn as it roared past; the rest of the small convoy followed suit. The mocking sounds dragged Holly kicking and screaming from her snug sensual cocoon. Little slivers of sense swam to the surface in her sex-saturated brain.

There was no leverage in the hands she ineffectually placed against his shoulders. 'This is very silly.' In broad daylight on the public highway—it was probably illegal, too!

His dark flushed face was very close to her own as she forced her eyes to open. The taut olive-toned skin was drawn tight across those impressive cheekbones. His eyes as he stared back at her were oddly unfocused.

'Definitely,' he agreed vaguely. The hands that slid underneath the short, semi-fitted silky shirt she'd hoped was suitable for meeting the aristocratic in-laws didn't seem very convinced.

He knew this was going to stop—he was going to stop. It wasn't as if this could go anywhere. His fingertips accidentally brushed the peak of one small breast and her body reacted as though she'd just suffered an electric shock; the deep ripple that passed through her entire body vibrated against the pads of his fingertips. He graphically pictured other, deeper ripples gripping that slender body. On the other hand, there was no big hurry, was there?

'Your skin is so incredibly soft!' he groaned, sliding his fingers over the slope of her ribcage just beneath the lacy bra she wore. Aroused beyond bearing, the constriction of his position became agonising as he breathed in the sweet, sharp, intensely feminine scent that arose from her hot skin and pictured her body beneath his.

The top buttons of her shirt had parted to reveal the shadowy promise of a very appealing cleavage. We are talking quality not quantity, here, he thought, recalling the pert outline of her small pointed breasts against that sexy dress she'd worn. With a groan, he pulled back; head pressed against the headrest, he dragged a slightly unsteady hand through his thick hair.

'You're right.' He turned his head to look at her. 'This isn't the time or place to do what we want.'

His assumption—understandable, possibly in the circumstances—made her eyes narrow. 'You're very free with the *we* all of a sudden.'

It was hard to sound haughty when her messed-up hair was sticking to her sweaty face and her shirt was unbuttoned all the way to her waist, but Holly was pretty plucky, not to mention stubborn. Niall Wesley kissed a girl and just assumed she was his—and, considering how well he kissed, she wasn't surprised he thought that way! But she wasn't going to be any man's casual lay! He was looking at his watch, that was how deeply involved he'd been!

'I'm probably not a gentleman to mention it, but you didn't act as if you were overcome with revulsion.'

'There's nothing wrong with your technique,' she conceded sneeringly.

'Why, thank you, ma'am.' He inclined his head mockingly in gratitude.

'That a little bit of spontaneity wouldn't cure.' Head on one side, she made a big show of giving the problem some consideration. 'Some of your moves seem a little stale, if you know what I mean…'

Irritatingly, he didn't seem the slightest bit hurt and offended. Head back, he laughed hard and long. Holly found there was something awfully appealing about the uninhibited way he gave himself up to mirth. You'd find something appealing about a wart, if he had one, she told herself angrily.

'I know *exactly* what you mean.' Holly didn't like the way he said that one bit. 'Don't worry, I'm never going to mistake you for anyone else, even with the lights off.'

Holly didn't quite know what to make of this ambiguous remark—it *might* be a compliment! Then again…

'I'm never likely to turn the lights off while you're around,' she hissed.

'Really?' His eyes widened appreciatively. 'How compatible we are, Holly. Though touch without the benefit of sight can be a very sensual experience, too. Yeah,' he speculated, warming to his theme, 'I rather like the idea of taking your hand and guiding you around my body.' His husky, indecent drawl summoned an erotic haze from clear air—it was so tangible she could have reached out and burnt herself on it.

'If you talk to me like that again, I'll—' she began explosively. Well, go on, what will you do, Holly? Lie down and say, Take me? 'I'll tell everyone we're not engaged.'

He smiled, not looking too worried by her threat. 'Well,

right now,' he said turning the key in the ignition, 'fasten up your shirt or I might just ruin my clean driving licence.'

Blushing wildly Holly did as she was bidden and lapsed into resentful silence. She was sure he was being sarcastic. It wasn't possible for a man who had had two such remarkably well-endowed women like Rowena and Tara in his life to find her less than ample curves worth driving into a tree.

Niall skirted the gravel-covered forecourt in front of the main entrance to his ancestral home and drove instead right around to the back of the house, where the Elizabethan origins of the great rambling building were very evident.

'Family barbecue,' he explained, holding the door open for her. 'And we're late.' His mother had a thing about lateness, which thirty-five years of being married to his absent-minded father had not dimmed.

Holly tore her eyes from the magnificent building he so casually called home and knew she couldn't even pretend to be at ease in these surroundings…with these people. She shook her head slowly from side to side.

'I can't do this, Niall.' She sat frozen with terror, glued to her seat. 'I thought I could but, now I'm here…'

'First night nerves?'

Holly clenched her chattering teeth. 'I'm a doctor, not an actor. Dinner with Tara is one thing…but your family…' Her voice trailed off unhappily. 'And you were no help. I didn't even know what clothes to bring,' she added shakily, nursing her resentment towards him.

'They're not royalty, you know; the country is crawling with impoverished baronets. I blame it on centuries of inbreeding, myself.'

'Your family isn't impoverished.'

'True,' he conceded, 'but you shouldn't hold that against

us. Mother's a farmer's daughter from solid, down-to-earth Irish stock, if that's any comfort.'

If his mother was a little green alien, it wouldn't alter the situation! 'It isn't.'

'Well it's too late to go all temperamental now, Holly. It sounds to me like someone's heard us arriving,' he said as the sound of a voice came closer. 'Come on; it'll be easy.' He grabbed her hand and pulled her physically from the Jag. Holly was catapulted against his chest. 'You might even enjoy yourself.'

'Sure, that's *very* likely,' she muttered, trying to push herself off a chest that had about as much give as a sheet of steel. Flickering images of an impressively muscled torso drifted distractingly before her eyes. 'Will you let me go?' she huffed breathlessly.

'No,' he told her, shifting his body so they were standing as if they were literally joined at the hip. The hand that had slid around her waist reached down and gave her bottom a friendly tap. 'We're probably being watched,' he told her, meeting her murderous glare with a determined teeth-clenched smile. 'And we need to present a picture of unity. First impressions, my *poppet*, are very important.'

Holly didn't give a damn about first impressions—she kicked him hard in the shin.

'Why, you little…!'

'I did warn you.'

Still rubbing his shin with the calf of his uninjured leg, he regarded her with a glittering smile that spoke very loudly of retribution. 'My mistake,' he conceded lightly. 'My nanny always taught me to respond to cruelty with kindness…'

'*Oh, no…!*' Holly cried, as she guessed what sort of kindness he had in mind. 'If you kiss me, my aim next time will be more accurate.' She just hoped this dire threat would have the desired effect.

Niall stopped and eyes narrowed regarded her angry flushed face with a curious expression. 'You would, wouldn't you?' There was the beginning of reluctant admiration in his voice.

CHAPTER FIVE

'IT LOOKS very much to me as if she would...' a drily amused voice behind Holly observed.

Holly spun around, her face ablaze with embarrassment.

'I've always said what my son needs upon occasion is a swift kick on the backside...' Her firm mouth quivered. 'Or thereabouts,' Maeve Wesley added reflectively.

Even though Niall's mother—because, with those eyes, she couldn't be anyone else—was taking the fact Holly had threatened her offspring with physical violence in very good part, Holly decided that now was probably a good time for the earth to open up and swallow her. She gave the grass beneath her feet a hopeful glance.

'It's great to meet a young woman who is like-minded.' Hand outstretched, the tall, vital figure moved forward.

Lady Wesley was nothing like Holly had expected. Tall and slim, handsome in a strong-boned way without being pretty, she looked remarkably youthful, despite the fact her dark hair was liberally streaked with grey.

'Hello,' Holly began weakly before stopping. What was she supposed to call her?

'Call me Maeve, and I shall call you Holly.' Her handshake was as firm and to the point as her manner. 'You're late, Niall.' She scowled disapprovingly at her son.

Niall smiled but didn't offer any explanations for their tardiness. He'd relaxed once he'd realised that his mother had interpreted the scene she stumbled upon as a lover's tiff—maybe, he mused thoughtfully, it was.

'Where's Tom?' he asked, impatient to see his son.

'With the other men, learning how to turn good food into charcoal, the last time I saw. He's still feeling the time difference after the flight,' she warned him. 'And you getting him overexcited on the phone last night didn't help much. It was hours before he eventually went to sleep.'

Niall, who'd felt pretty overexcited himself after the phonecall, smiled. 'We stopped to admire the scenery.'

The blush which had started to subside began to bubble once more as his mocking blue eyes swept over Holly's face.

'You! Since when did you enjoy the beauties of nature? I always thought you found inspiration inside a dirty, oily engine.'

'I'm expanding my horizons, mother.' This time, a microsecond of exposure to his eyes instantly turned Holly's bones to water. 'Come on, I want to see Tom.'

Holly, her stomach doing lustful acrobatics and with legs the consistency of jelly after that scorching scrutiny, obeyed the light touch on her shoulder and moved forwards. She didn't think simple *want* covered Niall's eagerness to see his son. Whatever else he was, Niall was obviously a very devoted father.

'And show off Holly of course.' The arm over her shoulders grew possessive.

Feeling suddenly deeply gloomy, Holly wondered what it would feel like to have that sentiment declared for real. A girl with her feet less firmly attached to terra firma might have been mesmerised by those beautiful lying eyes. She had to fight hard to subdue the urge to wrench herself free from his proprietorial grasp.

'You've changed your tune, all of a sudden.' Maeve turned her keenly intelligent look on Holly, who felt more convinced than ever that they'd never be able to pull this off. Nobody was going to think even for a second that she

was the sort of woman to attract Niall. 'You know, I had
to almost blackmail him to bring you along this weekend,
Holly.'

Blackmail obviously runs in the family, she thought di-
recting a dark look at his hawkish profile from under the
sweep of her gold-tipped lashes.

'It can be difficult. We can't plan our social life very
far ahead, with my awkward shifts. Niall is really very
good about being continually stood up at the last minute.'
In for a penny, she decided. As she threw caution to the
winds, she flashed a warmly intimate smile in Niall's general direction. Her eyes didn't stay still long enough to
register his reaction. 'Aren't you, darling?'

'Niall, patient?' His mother seemed to be nursing a private joke to herself. 'Yes, Tara did tell me you're a doctor.
I know I'm in danger of sounding ancient when I say this,
but you really do look too young.'

'I'm twenty-five.' Holly could see no point in holding
back the information her hostess was fishing for.

'Save the interrogation until later, hey, Mum?' Niall
suggested, his light tone held an audible note of firmness
as his grip on Holly, who didn't like the sound of that
later at all, tightened protectively.

Even though she knew he was protecting his own inter-
ests, not her, Holly felt a spurt of gratitude. She felt other
things she didn't really want to examine too deeply as his
fingers came to rest on the gentle curve of her hip.

They were only halfway along a narrow, winding, tree-
lined path when they walked headlong into the next con-
tingent of their reception committee.

One of the two small boys among them detached himself from the group and launched himself at Niall, who
automatically released Holly, squatted down to small boy
height and opened his arms wide.

'Dad! I've got heaps and heaps to tell you about. I saw whales—hundreds of them. I was sea-sick,' he added as a proud afterthought. 'And I can swim *nearly* as good as Dan now!'

'Enough…enough!' his father pleaded, laughing. 'I hope you've behaved for Aunty Jude and Uncle Chris.' He glanced warmly towards the waiting young couple. Holly saw that the woman looked like a younger and slightly softer copy of her mother and the man was very thin, very tall and wore wire-framed spectacles on a face that Holly instinctively warmed to.

The child's face became angelic in the extreme as he raised reproachful blue eyes to his father's face. 'They *enjoy* having me.'

'Sounds to me like you didn't want to come home…' The hell of it was, he was only half-teasing. The flash of insecurity had hit him out of the blue. If you looked at it logically, would it be so surprising if his son preferred living in a normal family group? Chris had taken the whole summer off to be with his family. Whereas I…! I must make more time.

'Well, it was great, but I sort of missed you.'

'Yeah, me too.' Niall returned the appealing grin. Despite the deficiencies of his parenting skills, the kid was turning out rather well. Wondering a little selfconsciously if he had 'besotted parent' emblazoned across his forehead, he ruffled his son's dark hair and stood up. He held out his hand to the tall man. 'Thanks, Chris.' His sister then received a quick hug. 'Is the baby sleeping the night through, yet?'

'Is that your idea of a joke?' Jude turned to Holly. 'Hi, you must be Holly.' Holly found the attractive brunette's friendly scrutiny a good deal less daunting than her mother's. 'I'm Niall's baby sister, Jude Appleby, and this is my husband Chris.'

There was understanding in Chris's kind eyes as he nodded in acknowledgement at Holly's tentative smile. 'An overwhelming lot, aren't they?' he said in a very attractive soft Transatlantic drawl. 'But you do get used to them.'

Holly knew she wouldn't be around long enough to get used to anything, except feeling a complete fake.

'If you've left your father alone with the food,' Maeve said, 'I suggest we save the introductions for a few moments or there'll be nothing to eat.'

Maeve Wesley seemed to Holly the sort of person who liked to organise things and people—especially people. She shot Niall a pleading look as his sister linked her arm in Holly's and started to chat in a friendly and open manner which Holly, more painfully conscious than ever of the fraud she was committing against these nice people, felt unable to respond naturally to. He winked unsympathetically at her and let his son drag him slightly ahead of the others.

Holly had a fresh surprise when they reached the broad sweep of well-manicured lawn that swept down from the house—well, Holly assumed it passed for a lawn, here; at home, they'd have called it a field—Tara was here too.

'Holly, how lovely to see you!' The blonde figure floated gracefully with every appearance of genuine pleasure towards her. The setting seemed perfect for her somehow. Dressed in a mini that showed off her stunning legs, she even outshone the peacocks in the beauty stakes. Obviously she hadn't spent hours figuring out what outfit wouldn't make her stand out like a sore thumb—she stood out quite beautifully.

Holly suspected her own response to the warm hug might have been more restrained if she really had been

Niall's fiancée. There couldn't be many women around confident enough to accept the presence of an ex-partner who looked so tiresomely gorgeous as Tara.

'I didn't know you'd be here.'

'Oh, yes, we're all one jolly extended family.' There was irony in Niall's deep voice as he came to stand behind Holly.

'Fortunately, we've got plenty of bedrooms here to accommodate my children's ex-partners…' Rubbing his hands on a striped apron Sir George Wesley, the chef, came towards them, having left the cooking to the younger generation. Holly saw immediately Niall had his father's impressive build and the family nose, but it was the similarity in their deep attractive voices that struck Holly most forcibly.

Rather than responding to his father's teasing challenge, Niall glanced anxiously towards his sister. Holly couldn't help but notice as her hand was firmly wrung that everyone else had glanced in Jude's direction, too.

'I'll just go and check on the baby,' Jude said, offering Holly a quick strained smile before she hurried, eyes lowered, off towards the house.

'Well, really, George!' his wife said in disgust.

'I didn't think!' Her spouse responded looking distinctly ill at ease. 'I wasn't even thinking about Jude. It was Niall I was—'

'Tell Judith that. I'll go and see how she is.'

Chris Appleby, quiet to this point spoke up. 'No, Maeve, I think she needs some time alone,' he said gravely.

Her mother didn't look convinced but, rather to Holly's surprise, she meekly did as her son-in-law suggested. Then, on reflection, she realised she wasn't really that surprised; despite the American's quiet unassuming air, he did have an aura of calm authority.

There was a definite tension in the air. She thought it a safe bet that she was probably the only person here who didn't have an inkling of what was going on. Fortunately, Thomas broke the awkward pause just in time—another two seconds and she'd have started babbling about the weather.

'Mum says you're a doctor.' He'd inherited the same electric blue eyes, and that disturbingly direct way of looking at a person, too. Give this tall gangly eight-year-old a few years and he'd be breaking as many hearts as his father.

'Yes, I am.'

'Are you Dad's doctor? Is he ill?' A small furrow creased the smoothness of his childish brow as he tried to puzzle out her presence.

'No, Tom, I'm not ill,' Niall reassured him lifting the dark hair flopping into his son's eyes. 'If you discount this nasty bruise on my shin…'

Nothing could have implied intimacy and shared secrets more than that little smile or the taunting challenge in his eyes as they touched her face. If she had smiled back in a besotted way, Niall would have assumed it was all part of the act, but Holly wouldn't permit herself this foolish weakness.

'I think,' Niall added critically, 'you could do with an appointment with a pair of scissors.'

'Is she your girlfriend, then?' The child persisted, refusing to be distracted.

'Yes, she is.'

'Oh, right.' His narrow shoulders lifted in an expressive shrug. 'I don't care what they say about ginger people,' he said, subjecting a deeply embarrassed Holly to a solemn scrutiny. 'I think she's *quite* pretty.' He ran over to his grandfather, who was urging the party to eat quickly before it started raining.

The adults hid their collective amusement—all barring Holly, who would have felt more relaxed if she'd just survived the Inquisition. She let out a long sigh of relief.

Niall bent down to speak softly in her ear. 'I must ask him what they do say about redheads.'

'Don't you feel even the slightest bit guilty?' she hissed.

'What for?'

'For lying to your family!'

'We lie every day of our lives—even you, Dr Parish— so put away that sanctimonious little smile and whip up some unquestioning adoration.'

'In your dreams!' she choked.

'Mine and every other male on the planet,' he conceded with a lecherous grin. 'If you want to make a hit with my father, just eat his food,' he advised, leading her towards the rest of the family, who had gathered around the table set under the rather grand picnic awning.

'I can't eat. I feel sick.'

'We'll all feel sick once we've consumed our token share of the burnt offerings,' he announced, with callous disregard for her mental torture. 'It'll be very handy to have a doctor in the house.'

Despite the age and grandeur of the historic house there was nothing museum-like about it. Primarily it was a home like every home, it had lots of small quirky individual touches that said things about the people that lived there. Holly kept telling herself this; she didn't want to give the impression she was awed by her surroundings—even if she was!

'Our bags have been taken up.' Niall appeared and she stopped gawking at the chandelier that was probably as big as their sitting-room, back home. 'Come on, I'll show you.' Without waiting for her, he started up the great sweeping staircase.

Holly decided it was lucky she was fairly fit, partly due to the fact she spent her life walking miles down hospital corridors, as Niall didn't make many concessions for the drastic difference in their inside leg measurements.

'This is the oldest part of the house.'

Holly nodded; she'd already noticed that the ceiling was a more intimate height in this, the original part of the building, that had begun life as a relatively modest Medieval manor house.

'Here we are.' He opened an oak-latched door with flourish and stood to one side as she entered.

'This is lovely.' It was a delightful half-timber panelled gem of a room: She'd seen bedrooms smaller than the vast fourposter that dominated it. She walked over to the window and gave an appreciative sigh. It looked out directly over the formal Italianate gardens and the lake beyond. Leaning her elbows on the stone sill, she poked her head out of the leaded frame to get a better view.

'Be careful!' A hand on her shoulder hauled her back.

The dizziness that afflicted Holly as she looked up into his dark face had nothing to do with vertigo. She ought to have added that she didn't need the support of the hand that encircled her waist, but somehow she didn't get around to it—it stayed there, light but disturbing.

Welcome distraction came in the form of a leather bag placed beside the awe-inspiring bed. 'They've brought the wrong bag up...or perhaps this isn't my room.'

His hand fell away as she took the opportunity to move away from him.

'I didn't say this was your room, I said this was *our*

room. That—' he nodded his head towards the offending item, '—is mine. So,' he added, his grin deepening, 'is that.' This time, his glance encompassed the massive four-poster.

Horror seeped slowly into Holly's brain. She shook her head slowly from side to side. What was he talking about? *Ours?* No, he'd said nothing about 'ours': it was something she'd definitely have noticed.

'Are you expecting me to share a room with you?' Her laughter, as she lifted a shaky hand to her head, was strained.

'It's not what *I'm* expecting: it's what my family is expecting. Mother prides herself on being very liberal and open-minded. From my point of view, I find musical beds to have a certain old-fashioned charm.' His casual smile had a lecherous quality that filled her with a fresh spurt of panic.

'You knew she'd put me in here,' she accused slowly. Then the truth dawned on her. 'Is this *your* room?'

'Man and boy,' he admitted solemnly.

'Why didn't you warn me?' she asked hoarsely.

'Aren't you overreacting just a bit?' The quirk of one dark brow casually trivialised her justified distress. 'If you'd actually paused to think about it, you'd have realised we'd be expected to share a bed—or at least a room.'

In her pale face, two feverish spots glowed hotly high on the curve of her smooth cheeks. 'Think about it?' she yelled in frustration, bringing both her fists to rest against his unyielding chest. 'That's what I've been trying not to do. This is a *nightmare*!' she groaned, bringing her chin to rest against her balled fists. As her fists themselves were still resting on his chest, her actions brought her inevitably into intimate contact with his well-toned torso.

Holly gasped and sexual heat, hot and fluid, rushed

through her body. Struggling against bonds that didn't exist outside the disgusted shock in her own mind, she staggered backwards—but not before she became aware that she wasn't the only one sexually aroused by the contact. Her belly quivered helplessly as she recalled the imprint of his hard sex against her.

Niall regarded her flushed face with an inscrutable expression. When he spoke, he didn't sound like a man driven to distraction by lust.

'We're only going to share a bed. Anything else is purely optional.' Looking into his burning blue eyes, Holly revised her estimation: not driven to distraction, possibly, but edgy...definitely edgy. If it was possible for eyes to reach out and grab a person, Niall had those eyes; she felt well and truly grabbed!.

She resisted the temptation to laugh scornfully at the idea of her voluntarily sharing a bed with him. Given the state of her hormones, the last thing she needed was him taking it into his head to make her eat her words!

'You should have warned me,' she persisted stubbornly.

'Some things are on a need-to-know basis, and you didn't need to know until absolutely necessary.'

'On what do you base that ridiculous comment?' she demanded hotly.

'On the basis that you would have given me earache,' he told her with breathtaking candour, 'earlier.' He parted the drapes around the bed—the heavy fabric was encrusted in jewel-coloured crewel work—and laid his holdall down. He withdrew a parcel wrapped in garishly coloured paper. 'Think you can find your own way back?'

Holly nodded untruthfully. Orienteering never had been her strong point. She would probably expire from thirst before she encountered another human being. The fact this notion wasn't nearly as worrying as the idea of sharing his bed told her she'd lost all sense of proportion…

'I want to spend some time with Tom.' He walked towards the door and then turned back his hand on the handle. 'She doesn't offer to give everybody the guided tour personally, you know.'

Left to her gloomy solitude, Holly assumed he was talking about his mother; she couldn't help wishing she wasn't so privileged.

'You'll know everyone there this evening except Ian Webster, he's the estate manager.' Niall glanced in the mirror as he knotted his tie.

Holly glared at his perfect profile and felt her sense of resentment grow—he made it sound so easy! She cinched the belt of her robe a notch tighter. 'I won't *know* anyone there tonight,' she corrected him resentfully. 'I'm the outsider…which is where incidentally I'd like to be—outside and far away from here.'

She'd managed to establish herself as a totally unsuitable bride for the heir to this estate during her guided tour. She didn't ride, she didn't shoot anything—not even clay targets—and she wasn't quite sure what had made her assure her hostess in a borderline belligerent manner that she had no intention of learning any of these skills. When his parents returned from their trip to the States and discovered their son was once more single and eligible, they'd no doubt breathe a collective sigh of relief.

'Try to be philosophical about this,' Niall advised, turning to look at her. He glanced at the outfit she'd laid out on the bed. 'That dress again…' A reminiscent smile played around the corners of his mouth.

'It's not like I have any choice,' she snapped. Unlike my sister and your glamorous ex-wife, she could have added, but she didn't; it might have made her sound petty and even jealous.

'We don't dress for dinner normally; it's just they don't have an opportunity to welcome someone new to the family every day of the week.'

'I'm not going to be one of the family.'

'Do you have to be so pedantic?' He held up his hand. 'No, don't answer that. You obviously can't help yourself.'

'Actually, your father gave the distinct impression it wasn't very unusual having…*guests*.' She wondered how often Rowena had been here. A nasty thought occurred to her. Had her sister slept in this very bed—and not alone?

Niall sighed. 'You noticed that, did you?'

Holly looked at the four-poster and wondered queasily. 'I noticed your sister seemed upset.' A bed is an inanimate object, she told herself; who has slept in it with whom is totally irrelevant. The important thing to remember is I'm not sharing it with anyone!

'Yeah, she was: not that the old man was getting at her.'

No, just his womanising son. Holly's expression hardened at this fresh reminder of Niall's reputation. It didn't make her feel more kindly disposed towards him.

'The thing is,' he explained slowly. 'Daniel isn't Chris's son. Jude got involved with a guy who turned out to be married. The hard-faced bastard had been here, smarming his way into everyone's good books, had the red carpet rolled out for him—even though he was years too old for Jude…' His expression was stony as he recalled the sequence of events that had had a permanent effect on his sister's life. 'Jude didn't find out until it was too late. Even then he strung her along, saying he'd leave his wife. He was hard to pin down to specific dates, you understand.'

Holly understood. Her dark eyes filled with compassion. 'Poor Jude.'

'She wasted three years of her life on the swine, and there was nothing any of us could do to stop her.' The stern line of his mouth was a bitter slash in his hard face. 'She had to learn the hard way.'

'But she met Chris.' She resisted the weird impulse to reach out to him.

Some of the grimness left his face as he smiled. 'Yeah, she met Chris,' he agreed.

'He seems nice,' she suggested carefully.

'One of the good guys. It wasn't a criticism.' He abruptly switched the subject and reached down to touch the silky fabric of her dress. Holly responded with a helpless shiver to the sight of his long shapely fingers caressing the material. She felt her tingling nipples harden brazenly under the thick towelling. 'Quality, not quantity,' he mused.

She saw a curiously self-conscious expression flicker across his face as he abruptly released the fabric and turned towards the window.

'I see Rowena has converted you to her way of thinking,' Holly observed sourly. 'A classic designer item is worth starving for? Actually, it was a gift.' She glanced at the offending article and didn't add that it wasn't an original.

Martin's mother ran a small firm that specialised in producing copies of designer originals worn by the famous. Martin's mother was doing very well; a lot of people, it seemed, were prepared to pay for their little bit of glamour at a price that wouldn't break the bank—just strain it.

'Rowena has excellent taste.'

Holly couldn't help but notice with a stab of anger how swift he was to defend her sister from possible criticism. Her lips tightened.

'It wasn't from her.' Suddenly she didn't want to be the

sort of woman who everyone assumed would only receive an expensive gift from her sister. Why shouldn't she have some wealthy, besotted lover hovering solicitously in the background? She ground her bare toes into the thick rug that partly covered the dark oak boarded floor.

Niall had turned back to face her; he was frowning critically. 'Some gift…Special sort of friend?'

'I did him a favour,' she responded, not much caring in her present frame of mind what Niall made of this deliberately obscure explanation. Where did he get off, anyway, with all that tight-lipped disapproval? It wasn't any of his business if she let a man shower her with diamonds! Her eyes were drawn to the large sapphire sitting on her finger.

She had thought Martin's gesture had been sweet. It wasn't as if she'd passed the Pharmacology resit for him; she'd just helped him out with his revision.

'He obviously had no complaints.'

'*He's* called Martin.' And she hadn't seen him since they qualified; she really ought to make more of an effort to keep in touch. Her frown deepened. She didn't like Niall's sneery, condescending tone one little bit.

'And what did *Martin* make of you coming here with me this weekend?'

This had gone far enough. Carrying off the pretence of having the odd lover hovering in the background might be a useful face-saving device, but she just didn't have the stamina or the bare-faced cheek to keep it up for long.

'I don't know. I didn't actually tell him. We don't really have that sort of relationship,' she confessed reluctantly.

'I see.' His next words made it pretty clear he didn't see at all. 'It's just hard luck on Martin, then, if he doesn't feel as casual as you.'

'Why are you yelling at me?' she asked with a mystified frown.

'I'm not yelling.'

'No, I'm sure you're far too well-bred to yell,' she accused hotly.

'Were they his pyjamas?'

'Who…what…?' She no longer had the faintest idea what he was talking about.

Niall didn't know what had possessed him to ask such a thing…only the ownership of the stripy pyjamas that had drowned her petite frame had been persistently bugging him. The furrow between his brows deepened. It wasn't like him to get diverted by irrelevant trivialities.

'The ones you were wearing the other morning,' he said gruffly.

Typical! He *would* remember what she was wearing when she looked a sight, wouldn't he? Mind you, he did recall the dress too and she hadn't looked a sight then…

'No, they weren't Martin's. If you must know, I'm too busy with work to have a regular boyfriend.'

'Just a string of casual acquaintances,' he suggested.

It was that faint curl of his sensual upper lip that made her see red. The sheer hypocrisy of his masculine condemnation—if I'd been a man, she thought angrily, he'd have been patting me on the back. The final irony was, of course, that she didn't have a sex life to speak about, let alone sneer about! It was just his nasty imagination providing the dirt in her whiter-than-white existence.

'It's a lot easier to part with a casual acquaintance—or even a string of them—than a husband or wife,' she pointed out tightly. Niall Wesley was in no position to offer her advice on relationships.

'So you and Rowena have that much in common, at least.'

Rowena didn't make any secret of the fact she had no intention of marrying.

'No, I can't even claim to have even that much in common with my sister. I've nothing against marriage, you see: I just think it shouldn't be taken as lightly as it seems to be by *some* people.' Her voice faltered. Niall was looking more remote and yes, *dangerous*, with each reckless syllable that passed her lips. 'When I do it,' she added in a small defiant voice, 'I want it to be forever.'

'A noble aspiration.'

'Spare me the cynical disillusion,' she pleaded unsympathetically. 'And I don't want it to happen for a long time yet—marriage, that is,' she added. 'I'm too young; I've too much to do,' She fretted defensively.

'You're older than I was when Tara and I got married.'

Holly's shoulders lifted. She couldn't help but notice that his jaw, never soft at the best of times, resembled steel by this point. 'Which rather proves my point, doesn't it?'

'And what happens to your grand plan if you meet someone, fall desperately in love—totally under his spell and he wants to marry you?' His voice had dropped to a low husky drawl that made a rash of goosebumps break out over her hot skin. Fighting with Niall always got her hot and bothered. 'He *insists* on marrying you.' The rough velvet voice persisted.

'If he really loved me, he'd wait.' A fine sheen of moisture broke out over her skin as she tried to drag her eyes away from his mesmeric gaze.

'Maybe he doesn't love you—maybe he just *wants* you. You're the one in love. You're totally in his power, and you like it.'

For one split second of mind-numbing panic, she thought he was actually accusing her. Simultaneously, she knew that accusation would be true! The man she loved was never going to insist on marrying her. He probably wouldn't mind sleeping with her, if there was nothing better to do.

'I wouldn't be so stupid,' she scoffed bravely.

'Haven't you ever wanted to please someone so badly that you can't think about anything else?'

The husky question shook her more than anything else he'd said. There was derision and something else much more scary in his intent gaze.

'You're talking as if you have a choice,' he continued. 'Love isn't like that…'

You could say that again! She moistened her dry lips with the tip of her tongue and scanned his handsome, relentlessly cruel face with a kind of helpless fascination. Loving this man was not something she'd choose to do—loving Niall was a disaster! God, she didn't want him telling her what love was like for him….That was more than she could bear!

'…didn't you know that, Holly?'

She stopped the small agitated pants that made her slight bosom rise and fall dramatically and took a deep steadying breath. 'You're talking about lust not love!' she jeered shakily. Desire so intense, so *basic* flooded through her; she felt weak. 'Love is about mutual respect.'

'True, but it's also about sex.'

Holly was worried her knees were about to give way. 'Were you in love when you married Tara?' she croaked, missing jeer and sounding just plain scared.

Niall blinked and snapped back up to his full overpowering height. She hadn't been conscious until that moment how closely, how intimately his big body had been curved towards her. She didn't think at first he was going to reply to the question that had been motivated more by need to distract him than a desire for a reply—she already knew the answer.

'Blindly in love,' he told her flatly. With an emphasis on the 'blind'. Now he could look back on the embarrassing memory of his youthful romantic idealism and see the numerous warning signs that should have made him back off.

And now? she wanted to ask, but didn't. She suspected she knew that answer, too.

Holly scooped up her clothes and turned towards the bathroom. 'I won't be long,' she mumbled.

CHAPTER SIX

HOLLY soon learnt that tact wasn't Sir George Wesley's middle name.

'Rowena's sister, eh? A *fine*-looking girl, Rowena.' His eyes lit up as he thought about Holly's sister. 'Extraordinarily fine. You're not a bit like her.' He looked benignly around, obviously expecting his view to be endorsed.

Several totally unrelated conversations broke out simultaneously to cover the awkward pause. This wasn't the first time Holly had heard unfavourable comparisons, and not all had been as unmalicious as her host's.

She looked from George Wesley, his expression bemused and irritated, to the others around the table, all busy being deaf, and her sense of humour came to her rescue. She burst out laughing. Soon, she wasn't alone.

'She'll need a sense of humour with you, Niall,' his sister laughed, dabbing the corners of her eyes with a tissue.

Niall hadn't joined in the general merriment at his father's expense but he was faintly smiling as he looked at the woman wearing his ring on her finger. Holly felt his eyes; she turned her head. Something about that enigmatic smile made Holly's heart thud painfully fast. Nervously, she twisted the white linen napkin into a tight ball in her lap.

'Why should she take offence?' a bewildered George Wesley asked, in reply to his wife's hissed complaint. 'She's a very nice-looking little thing, but the sister's a stunner.'

'Yes, she is, isn't she?' Holly agreed calmly, taking pity on him.

'There, you see.' He looked around the table with an injured expression. 'And Maeve tells me you're a medic.'

Holly nodded. 'I've not been qualified long.'

'There's a lot of money to be had in doctoring.'

'Not in the field I'm interested in,' Holly admitted ruefully.

'And what field might that be?' Her host's expression suggested he was slightly shocked by her lack of avarice.

'Community medicine. It doesn't have the glamour of some specialities—'

'Cosmetic surgery, that's what you want,' George Wesley recommended in his abrupt way. 'How old was Emily's daughter when she had her boobs done...nineteen? They're all at it, you know.'

Niall, who had been knowledgeably discussing the pros and cons of organic farming with Ian Webster, broke off at this point to make his contribution to her embarrassment.

'Not quite *all*, Father, I'm happy to say.'

His smile suggested he was contemplating something very pleasant; the direction of his gaze gave a giant clue as to what the pleasant thing was.

It took all her will-power not to peek down to check that her meagre bosom was still adequately covered. Niall had a way of looking at her that made her feel stark naked. She wasn't sure how much longer she could endure this conversation.

'Well, you ask Quinn if you don't believe me. Friend of Niall went in for that field, my dear,' he told Holly. 'Made quite a name for himself. He's raking it in. You should talk to him; he'd put you right.'

'Quinn Tyler.' Holly nodded. 'Yes, I know him.'

Watching the little smile that played about her lips made Niall feel vaguely disgruntled. 'How do you come to know Quinn?'

'Charming rogue,' Maeve observed, ignoring her son's abrupt, accusing contribution to the discussion. 'I like him.'

'*Charming*? That's a polite way of putting it,' Niall responded with austere distaste.

Holly turned to stare at him with incredulous disbelief. When it came to broken hearts, she was sure Niall had left just as many in his wake as Quinn.

'I like him, too.' Holly smiled at her hostess before turning her attention back to Niall. She was still a trifle puzzled by his cranky behaviour...Perhaps he and Quinn had had some sort of falling out. Both were pretty thick with Rowena. Were they rivals for her affections?

'I hardly think you're in a position to throw the first stone, Niall. Come to think of it, you're in no position to throw the last!'

Niall's father chuckled. 'That's right, girl, you tell him.'

Niall cast a withering look in the direction of his father. 'You still haven't told us how you come to know Quinn.'

'I haven't told everyone else because *they* don't particularly want to know.' Why did he persist in acting as though she was being deliberately evasive? 'I know Quinn the same way I know you—obviously.'

The dubious fringe benefit of being Rowena's little sister was meeting gorgeous men who would never otherwise cross her path. Life would have been much simpler if one particular gorgeous man hadn't crossed her path, she thought gloomily!

'Not *that* well, hopefully.'

This loaded comment was obviously meant for their audience and it reminded Holly that she had to stay in character.

'Rowena told Quinn I wanted to go to medical school and he was really helpful. He's kept in touch.'

'You never mentioned that.'

Holly was so startled by the tone of his observation, she forgot once more the part she was playing. 'Why on earth should I?' she asked in genuine bewilderment.

'Yes, Niall,' Jude prompted. 'Why should she?' The grin she exchanged with her husband was brimming with amusement. 'We live and learn,' she said, softly, leaning towards her brother. 'I never had you pegged as the jealous type.' Those sitting close to them heard the comment and responded with indulgent expressions.

Niall's expression was not brimming with brotherly love as he chose to ignore Jude's gentle taunt.

A wave of mortification washed over Holly. I'm so slow, she silently berated herself; he was *playing* the possessive lover! For one moment there she'd thought maybe…*Stop it!* Daydreams are out, she reminded herself.

'He's not jealous,' Holly contradicted in a firm voice. She was gratified to see the flicker of concern on Niall's face. She paused for a moment, letting him wonder whether he'd pushed her too far. 'He just likes winding me up.'

'Well actually, Holly—' Tara's voice could be clearly heard over the general murmur of amusement '—I think you enjoy winding him up, too,' Tara revealed with alarming accuracy. Her sweet smile made it impossible to take offence.

Was anything more stimulating than a battle of words with Niall? There was, and that involved Niall as well; just thinking about it made Holly want to hide under the table. The thought was so vivid, and came with such explicit mental pictures, she didn't see how anyone could *not* know what wicked ideas were drifting through her mind.

Niall raised his crystal goblet to his ex-wife but his eyes were on Holly. 'To your insight,' he complimented Tara. 'And now, because I know you don't like it, we won't squabble. Will we, my love?' he purred.

A heavy dragging sensation twisted her stomach muscles into knots as, dry-throated, she stared back. The seductive swine, she inwardly raged. Did he have any idea what it did to her when he looked at her like that?

She tossed her head. 'That depends on how reasonable you're going to be.'

Of course he knew! Niall Wesley was callous and calculating and he left *nothing* to chance when it came to getting what he wanted. That sort of begs the question…Does he want me—*really* want me? And can I accept what he's offering? More to the point, can I refuse? *Do I want to refuse?*

Niall refrained from any further dramatic displays of the jealous lover throughout the evening. No, she thought bitterly, he's already established our roles to his satisfaction—and everyone else's, it would seem. She encountered none of the scepticism she'd expected and she was frankly amazed by their ready acceptance of her and the role she was playing.

'What exactly are you doing?' Niall pulled his loose tie free; it fell unheeded to the ground when he flung it carelessly towards a chair.

Cool, firm but don't lose your sense of humour—and *definitely* don't get defensive, Holly told herself severely. He's not stupid; he'll guess straight off that I'm having a hard time keeping my hands off him. She took a deep steadying breath. She continued to drape the blanket over the small sofa set in the deep alcove beneath the window. 'What does it look like?' she snapped, forgetting her game plan the instant she looked at him standing there so relaxed, so starkly, mouth-wateringly gorgeous!

'I hope you're not expecting me to sleep on that, because if you are...'

She straightened up and let her scornful gaze rest on his tall figure. 'I'd hardly expect *you* to do the chivalrous thing.'

'I'd call sleeping in that thing when there's a perfectly good bed—which could comfortably accommodate half a dozen people, let alone two—stupid, not chivalrous.'

'Half a dozen!' Holly echoed, releasing a low whistle of derisive admiration. 'When you said your mother was liberal I didn't think you meant *that* liberal.'

'I never really put her open-mindedness to the test, at least not in that direction,' he corrected drily. 'Although, for all I know, my ancestors might well have held orgies in this very room...this very bed...' he conceded smoothly. 'I've just had to control any inclinations I might have towards wholesale debauchery while under the parental roof.'

Holly's gasped, casual discussions of orgies had spooked her badly; her skin prickled and her slender frame tensed as she looked with dismay towards his lean dark face. There was something quite scarily predatory about the look in his eyes. She inched a little farther away from the big bold bed as if she might somehow be infected by the lax morals of previous times. Deep down, she knew it was her own morals she was worried about—or, rather, lack of them just now.

'I'll feel more comfortable here,' she told him primly.

Niall came across the room and bent down to test the

stuffed seat with his hand. 'I seriously doubt that,' he responded wryly as he straightened up to his full intimidating height. 'When they restored this thing, they had authenticity in mind, not comfort.'

'I don't mind…'

'Stoicism is such an overrated virtue, don't you think?' He yawned.

'How was Tom?' she asked, ignoring his heavy sarcasm.

'Asleep.' His expression sobered. 'Some days that's the only time I see him.' Holly could hear the dissatisfaction and self-recrimination in his deep voice. She watched warily as he sat down on the sofa and impatiently pushed the pillow she'd filched from the bed onto the floor.

She picked up the pillow and clutched it to her chest. It disturbed her deeply to feel such an immediate surge of empathy for his distress. Still nursing the pillow, she moved towards the sofa and fell to her knees on the rug.

'A lot of parents with busy work schedules must have the same difficulty, especially single ones.' Then, strongly conscious of Niall's protective attitude towards the mother of his child, she hurried on, 'I'm sure Tara is a great mum, but you carry the main responsibility, and I suppose you must be doing something right.'

Niall's head lifted from its recumbent position against the back of the sofa and he looked curiously at her from under the extravagant sweep of his jet-black lashes. He might well wonder at the impulse which drove her to offer him comfort, she reflected; she was wondering herself!

'He seems a nice, well-balanced kid.' She felt ridiculously selfconscious and wished she had kept her mouth safely shut. She gave a nervous little laugh. 'He must take after his mother,' she joked weakly. Why was he looking at her in that curiously intense way?

'Anyway, if you were still racing, you'd see a lot less of him,' she pointed out fairly.

'It was the fact I might not see him at all that made me jack it in,' he revealed surprisingly.

'Oh, is that why…?' she exclaimed. The satirical quirk of one dark brow made her subside, blushing in embarrassment at her gauche unthinking response. 'That is…I did wonder,' she told him with a hint of defiance. 'You didn't offer any explanations at the time.'

No, nothing so simple for Niall Wesley. The newspapers could vilify him as much as they liked and it would never have occurred to this pigheaded, self-sufficient man to do anything as simple as explain himself. He'd probably told his close friends, she reflected. People who wouldn't blab to the tabloids—people like Rowena. She felt a deep sharp pang that she wasn't numbered amongst this select band and never would be.

'I liked racing, but it wasn't my life…Well, no that's not strictly true,' he wryly came clean. 'It probably *was* my life until Tom was born. Afterwards, I wanted to see him grow up,' he told her simply. 'I didn't want to do anything to deliberately narrow the odds of that happening. I'm not saying I had a suicide mentality before that, but I didn't lose any sleep worrying over my mortality—even, I'm ashamed to say, when poor Tara repeatedly begged me to quit.'

'She *wanted* you to quit…?' Another theory bites the dust, she thought, staring at him weakly. The media had insisted that his wife had deserted him because he'd quit the glamorous world of a Formula One driver.

'She hated me racing.'

Holly had a sudden image of him hurtling at ridiculous speed around the track, encased in a fragile pile of metal, and she shuddered. She pressed her chin hard into the soft feather pillow.

'I don't blame her.' Her words vibrated with husky sincerity that seemed to echo around the room. 'No doubt wanting to stay alive deprives you of your competitive edge.' She hoped her cynicism would counterbalance her initial response.

'You're probably right.' He dragged a hand through his dark hair and leant forwards, his lean fingers curling into the pillow she held tightly. 'We've sort of moved away from the subject, Holly.'

'What subject was that?' she asked, playing dumb for all it was worth as he firmly peeled the concealing layer of pillow from her chin.

'Sleeping arrangements.'

'Subject closed.' The prim line of her mouth quivered ever so slightly when she encountered his eyes; just beneath the surface humour there was a throat-drying, knee-trembling *sizzle*.

'Are you sleeping with Quinn Tyler? Is that why you're holding me off?'

The hard question came so totally out of the blue, she could only stare at him. *'Quinn?'*

'Because if that is the case, I have to tell you that your loyalty is misplaced,' he told her in a cold voice. 'If the situation were reversed, he wouldn't do the same. Take my word for it—I *know* Quinn.' There was hard, cynical light in his eyes.

'With a friend like you, a man doesn't have to go out looking for enemies, does he?' she gasped. 'Do you always slag him off?' Her expression grew suspicious. 'Or has he done something to annoy you?'

'I'm not saying anything to you I wouldn't say to Quinn's face.'

'My choice to not share your bed has nothing to do with Quinn.'

'You haven't answered my question,' he said, looking at her from narrowed eyes.

'Noticed that, did you?' she breathed with a sweetly provocative smile. 'Makes you think, doesn't it, that it could have something to do with the fact that it's none of your damned business who I sleep with?'

God, it was ironic that he seemed to think she had a whole legion of casual lovers. Whereas in reality, since her first never-to-be-forgotten disastrous introduction to the mating game, she'd led a nunlike existence. It was mortifying to acknowledge that in those days she'd been so pathetically grateful and flattered by the first plausible man who had said he wanted her that she'd imagined herself deeply in love.

She'd woken up when she'd discovered he'd used the same identical lines that had temporarily enslaved her with at least four other students she knew; *they'd* laughed at his corny chatup skills. Did it make it worse that in the end it turned out she wasn't the only gullible idiot? He'd been bedding at least two other equally naive girls at the same time as her!

'If it's me, it is.'

Holly lost her balance and her crouched position as his words registered. She ended on her modestly upholstered behind, gawping up at him.

'It won't be.' Her hoarse words didn't carry as much conviction as she'd have liked. 'I know I'm substituting for Rowena, but I'm not prepared to go all the way,' she told him, resorting to crudeness. She felt the sour taste of bitterness rise up in her throat.

Niall, it seemed, could cope with crudeness and respond in kind. 'Earlier on in the car, I got the distinct impression that that was *exactly* the destination you had in mind.' He watched the colour seep dramatically from her remarkably creamy skin.

Holly felt dizzy as this sly little reminder ricocheted around in her head. 'I suppose,' she sneered distantly, 'it was only a matter of time before you brought that up.'

'Glad to see you appreciate the restraint I've displayed so far.'

Holly gritted her teeth at his self-congratulatory tone. 'Ever the little gentleman.'

Niall shook his head slowly from side to side. His lean fingers curled firmly around her slender wrists as he drew her back up to her knees, until her body was within the strong barrier of his thighs.

'Compliments will get you nowhere, sweetheart,' he rasped against her ear as he placed her hands firmly around his neck. 'I've been wanting to do this...'

Holly gasped as one large capable hand tugged down the bodice of her slinky, shimmering gown. He gave a deep satisfied purr of pleasure as his eyes moved greedily over the flushed, heaving contours of her small bosom. Her heart pounded against the confines of her narrow ribcage as desire, hot and sweet, flooded through her entire body. The flood of heat between her trembling thighs made her weak and hopelessly needy. Did it matter that Niall didn't love her? He *needed* her, didn't he? And by God she needed him!

'...since the first time I saw you wearing this. Sweet little witchy woman. Do you taste this good all over?' he enquired, lifting his head from her neck and looking at her with passion-glazed, smoky blue eyes.

His fingers brushed against the youthfully resilient firm flesh on the outside of her right breast before his thumb touched the aching, hard, rosy bud. Holly gave a deep anguished whimper of pleasure as the contact sent ripples of pleasure through her entire body.

He pushed his fingers into the fiery nimbus of curls that covered her head and examined her dreamily aroused face with hungry eyes. 'That's it!' he declared decisively. 'There's no way you're sleeping on this thing tonight.'

His arrogant certainty stirred the last stubborn dregs of her resistance. 'Says who?' The lustful thrust of his tongue into the warm welcome of her mouth destroyed any last shreds of sanity she had left.

Mouth still attached to hers, he lifted her into his arms and walked towards the bed. They were inches away from their destination when he encountered the unexpected obstacle of one spikily heeled sandal she'd carelessly kicked off when she'd first entered the room.

He let out a sharp curse as he tripped and they were both catapulted headlong onto the bed. The impetus drove them through the partly drawn drapes and straight onto the bed. Holly's light body sank deep into the soft mattress. She was so lost to decency and consumed by lust that it flickered wickedly through her head that she wouldn't have minded at all if it had driven Niall deep into her! It didn't; at the last second, with a display of startling co-ordination and reflexes, he managed to take his weight on his braced arms.

'Sorry. Are you all right?' he asked anxiously as he pushed the thick curtain of copper curls from her face.

'F-fine.' Breathless didn't begin to cover her condition. She made an ineffectual and, under the circumstances, deeply silly attempt to pull down the skirt of her dress, which had rucked up around her middle. How fortunate someone had thought to turn the bed down, she thought irrelevantly, when she realised she was lying on soft sheets.

Niall rolled away from her, which she found was something she didn't entirely approve of. She'd rather enjoyed it when, hands either side of her head, knees tucked snugly up against her thighs, her world had been dominated by a close-up view of his awesomely powerful body.

'A shoe.' He turned accusingly back to her.

Holly propped herself up indignantly on one elbow, an action which caused the bodice of her dress to slither all the way down to her waist. 'It's not my fault you weren't looking where you were going!'

A smile tugged at the corner of his mouth as amusement crept into his eyes. Looking at his mouth, all Holly could think of was how firm his lips had been, how velvety smooth and skilful his tongue had been; dreamily, she ran her tongue over her dry lips, still able to taste him.

The sultry but artless gesture made Niall's eyes darken. The inky blackness of his pupils expanded to almost obliterate the electric blue. He let his eyes drop to wander obviously over her semi-naked body. It made the ache in his groin intensify to critical levels to see the way her nipples hardened and swelled. And he was just looking: if he *touched*…She was so incredibly sensitive, the possibilities were endless…

Her belligerent face was flushed and she was breathing hard and fast by the time his eyes reluctantly shifted from their lengthy contemplation.

'You wouldn't let me breathe, let alone look where I was going.'

'Are you saying there's something wrong with the way I kiss?'

'Do I look like a fool?' He saw her expression and shook his head. 'Pretend I didn't say that?' he pleaded with a wry smile. 'You kiss like an angel—the fallen variety,' he reflected with a deep, very flattering sigh. 'But you're a bit of a slob on the neatness front. However, I'm prepared to take full responsibility, if it will make you feel happier,' he offered generously.

'I'm perfectly capable of taking responsibility for my own actions,' Holly told him, with a brave attempt at haughtiness. Anticipation was sliding through her, stretching each fine muscle fibre in her slender body so tight, it hurt—wanting to touch Niall hurt.

Abruptly Niall dropped down beside her and hauled her towards him until they lay there, thigh to thigh; the similarity ended there. Her thigh was slim and softly rounded; his was hard and, even through the dark fine wool of his trousers, visibly muscled. She wanted badly to reach out and feel how hard his body was. Holly had never dreamt that such obvious contrasts could be such a major turn-on.

'I'm glad to hear it.' His eyes as they sought hers were unexpectedly sombre. 'And you're sure…about *this*…?'

'It doesn't sound as though you are!' she responded, perversely annoyed by this display of caution. She was way past caution; she'd entered the realms of inevitability.

He leant over and gently pressed his face into her burnished hair. *'Oh, I'm sure.'* To Holly's sensitive ears, he sounded pretty grim about it.

He shrugged off his formal jacket and discarded this fine example of bespoke tailoring carelessly. Midway down his chest, the buttons of his shirt had come adrift; she could see the interesting sprinkling of dark hair against delicious firm, olive-toned skin.

Holly tucked her tongue between her clenched teeth— it would look bad if she actually started slobbering. He flinched as she placed a curious finger against the bare warm flesh and then, taking her wrist in one hand, he used the other to impatiently flick the remaining buttons free. Spreading her fingers, he placed them flat against his chest.

'Is that what you want to do?' he grated.

Want? Her vocal cords had seized up completely. She nodded her head vigorously. 'Want' hardly seemed an adequate description for the swirl of conflicting sensations that ripped through her as she touched his skin and heard the deep vibration of his steady heartbeat beneath her fingertips. She felt so much, it scared her; emotion brought a sheen of hot tears to her dark eyes as she gazed at her own hand, very pale against his darker skin. She was almost too frightened to move her fingers.

'Among other things,' she confided huskily, with a sly, sultry peek up at him from under the sweep of her copper-tipped lashes.

Niall swallowed. *'Other things,'* he purred. 'You interest me greatly. Tell me more…' he encouraged throatily, placing two strong hands either side of her narrow hips and drawing her hard against the straining swell of his restricted manhood.

'Stop talking,' she pleaded hoarsely, 'and just kiss me!'

Niall's vibrant laugh was one of male triumph and delight as he did his best to obey her imperious command. His best was pretty good!

'Oh, gosh!' she gasped when he finally lifted his head. She felt well and truly ravaged—no, she decided wiping the sheen of sweat from her brow, *beautifully* ravaged! 'I thought I was in love with you, when I was sixteen.' Her tingling lips felt tenderly swollen as she ran the tip of her tongue along the outline.

Niall exhaled sharply as his eyes followed the tiny gesture. He half levered himself up and ripped the shirt from his back. 'I know.'

'I knew you knew,' she murmured in a distracted voice. His impressive rippling torso, all hard sinew, firmly sculpted muscles and smooth satiny skin, was deeply distracting. She didn't need medical training to know she was looking at perfection. 'It was very humiliating,' she confided frankly. 'Of course, I've been over it—you—for years and years.' Now wasn't the time to reveal what a catastrophic relapse she had had—there probably never would be a good time for that!

'Feel better now you've firmly established the fact you're not in love with me?'

Holly knew that the clipped tone in his voice was somehow significant, but the realisation slipped away from her as his hands began to move ever so softly over the rigid peaks of her engorged breasts. Her nerve-endings formed new and marvellous connections as her entire body came alive. The ache between her thighs became more acute.

'No,' she lied unselfconsciously. 'Just ever so slightly in lust.' She arched her back as he knelt over her and, threading one arm through the curve in her lower back, hauled her relaxed body upright until her face was on a level with his.

'Your frankness, little one, could wound a lesser man.'

Holly looped her arms around his neck and plastered her naked upper half against him, squirming to get maximum contact from the manoeuvre. She gave a gusty sigh of deep pleasure—he felt quite marvellous. 'All right,' she conceded with a sigh. 'At this moment, a lot in lust!'

The sombreness lifted from Niall's face to be replaced by a fierce hunger as he laughed out loud. 'You never say what I expect you to.'

'Is that a good thing?' she purred throatily. His eyes were incandescent as they scanned her aroused face.

The fact that this perfect sample of rampant maleness was shaking—fine tremors were visibly running through his greyhound-lean frame—made her feel suddenly strong and in charge. I'm irresistible, men are putty in my hands:

it was a very potent delusion. It lasted all the way up to his next kiss, which was frenzied and urgent, she felt the salty tang of blood on her tongue.

'Let's get you out of these, shall we?'

Holly closed her eyes as he lay her down. She hoped he wasn't expecting any help, because she was incapable—incapable of lifting a finger. Incapable too of rational thought, or any thought at all, save the blind mating instinct that told her this was the man she was meant to be with forever. Tragedy was, he didn't know about the forever part, so she'd have to settle for now—and now he was hers!

After he'd peeled the last scrap of clothing from her trembling body—fortunately, he hadn't needed any assistance—he stopped…Stopped touching her, stopped talking: she might even have suspected he'd stopped breathing if she hadn't been able to hear the harsh sound of his laboured exhalation.

'You're incredible.'

It didn't sound like a casual compliment; it had more bite, more *guts* to it. As her eyes flickered open, she didn't doubt for one minute his husky sincerity. His eyes captured and held hers as he reached down and firmly parted her pale thighs. He slowly ran his fingers along the inner aspect of her legs from ankle to thigh, making her moan with pleasure. When he came to the damp curls at the apex of her legs and he touched her there, her low cry became sharp and feral and her arched body cleared the bed for that split second when every muscle in her body tightened and screamed out for fulfilment.

His head was against her breasts, teasing each aching inch of flesh with long, tantalising strokes of his tongue. As he suckled, his hands slid between her aching thighs and she was just too stunned by the force of her own response, her own pleasure and need, to do anything but sob his name.

'Niall…I…I need…' Her hands clutched at his sweat-slick shoulders, sliding over ridges of hard muscle.

'It's all right, my lovely little witch.' Despite the stamp of desire that drew the olive skin hard against his prominent cheekbones, there was surprising tenderness in his face as he caught her chin in one hand and angled her face up towards him.

'I need the same…Feel.' He guided her hand towards the proof of this claim. Her hand curled greedily over him. The zipper of his trousers dug into the bulging ridge of his arousal, making it hard for her to release. He made no attempt to help her and this somehow heightened her frenzied clumsy desire.

'Oh, God!' she gasped when she'd succeeded. 'You're…' Her eyes felt hot and heavy and they were transfixed. It probably wasn't the done thing to stare, but she couldn't seem to stop.

His grin had a wolfish cast as he kicked his boxers free. 'Hurting. I'm hurting, Holly.'

'I think I know a cure.' Heart in her eyes, she held out her hand.

Niall retained the grip on her hand as his body covered hers. Her fingernails dug into his palm as, with a powerful but controlled thrust, he slid inside her.

'Don't stop!' she pleaded, as her body welcomed the extraordinary feeling of fullness.

His laugh was strained as the taut line of his clenched jaw. 'Even if I wanted to, I couldn't!'

Holly stared up at the elaborate hangings above her head. She was very, *very* glad he hadn't stopped. There was still a deep warm glow where he'd been, low down in her belly, and tiny aftershocks that were faint echoes of that wild cascade of deep rippling contractions still fluttered every so often.

'You're not asleep?' A hand lifted the heavy damp hair from the nape of her neck.

It was the first time he'd spoken since he'd said her name. Even the memory of that wild triumphant cry could bring the fine downy hairs over her body erect.

She lifted her head from his chest and smiled, a sleepily content look. 'No.'

'Why not?'

'Not sleepy.' Holly gently teased the dark hairs across his chest, before she rolled onto her back and stretched, a smile of smug complacency on her full lips. She had something now that nobody could take away from her; her lips firmed into a defiant line. 'How about you?' she challenged recklessly. What am I asking for, she wondered, marks out of ten?

Niall grinned and rolled onto his belly. Head on one side, he subjected her to a thoughtful look which made the colour start to bloom hotly in her cheeks. Why did I ask that? The man had probably lost interest. That'll teach me to get pushy!

He traced a line from the base of her flat belly up through the gentle valley between her breasts, until it came to the pulse spot at the base of her neck. The fascinated expression on his face suggested he'd not lost interest, after all.

'It just so happens that I'm not tired either.'

'It makes me very happy to hear that,' she confessed with a sultry smile of approval.

'I'm about to make you a lot happier,' Niall predicted confidently.

CHAPTER SEVEN

'THEY can't have gone far, Jude,' Chris Appleby reassured his wife with a comforting air of certainty.

'They obviously got tired of waiting for Niall when he didn't come down to breakfast.' Her face white with anxiety, Jude's words were addressed to her brother, but her glare and likewise her animosity were reserved for Holly.

Jude's attitude had made it quite clear the second Holly had entered the room, blissfully unaware up to that point that Tom and his cousin hadn't been seen for two hours, that she blamed Holly for her brother putting his personal pleasure ahead of his paternal responsibilities.

Holly didn't think it could have been much more humiliating if they'd been asked to give a detailed account of what had been important enough to make Niall forget his promise to take the boys fishing this morning. To her guilty eyes, it seemed that everyone was looking at her with varying degrees of the same reproach.

How Niall must now regret carrying her back to their still-warm bed earlier. Suddenly, their early morning love-making had been transformed from something spontaneous and rather special into something grubby and sordid.

'Leave it alone, Jude,' Niall put in harshly.

Holly couldn't decide if he was actually defending her from his sister's wrath or just impatient that Jude was distracting them from the task in hand. He probably agreed with Jude! Why else did he seem to be avoiding her eyes?

'They were last seen in the stables, right?'

'Yes, your mother had just come back from exercising

Blue Boy.' George Wesley clapped his son on the shoulder. 'Chris is right, you know; the little devils can't have gone too far. I think half the problem,' he reflected, 'is that youngsters are just too coddled these days, wrapped in cotton wool. They need a bit of freedom without adults breathing down their necks. Why, when you two were young, you ran wild... *wild*! Do you remember the time when Niall here cracked his skull climb—?'

Maeve Wesley, whose memories of the occasion were composed almost entirely of sitting by her eldest child's hospital bedside, waiting to see if his brain had survived the accident unscathed, didn't share her husband's rosy view of the occasion; she nodded warningly.

'Yes, well, as fascinating as your ideas on childrearing are, my dear, I don't think now is quite the time.' She took hold of her husband's hand and pulled him firmly back to her side.

'We'll divide up to search. If we don't find them in the first half hour, we'll fetch in reinforcements. You take the stables, Chris, and I'll...'

Holly stood quietly to one side as Niall divided up the family and willing household staff into search parties. A surprisingly calm Tara was asked to keep a distraught Jude company; it seemed that Holly was the only one that hadn't been included.

'What can I do?' She caught hold of Niall's sleeve as he was about to sweep from the room. 'Can I come with you?'

Holly winced; the breathless request smacked uncomfortably of entreaty. His eyes didn't light up at the prospect of her sticking to his side like superglue—had she really thought it would? she asked herself derisively. It was obvious his thoughts were elsewhere. The rejection hurt but Holly didn't resent his preoccupation; she understood it.

His child had disappeared, so the man was bound to be a bit distracted. She ached to help alleviate his anxiety, but it was pretty obvious it hadn't occurred to him to look in her direction to do anything of the sort.

'You don't know the area, Holly. It's probably better if you stay here.'

Why should she mind being treated like an outsider? She *was* an outsider. Had she really thought sleeping with the man was some sort of magical formula? It wasn't going to transform what they had into something more deep and meaningful, she told herself with scalding self-derision.

'I'd probably slow you down.' The empty feeling in the pit of her churning stomach had nothing to do with the fact she'd missed her breakfast.

Her presence wasn't making things easier for Jude, so Holly quietly excused herself. She didn't blame the other woman; it was only natural that she needed someone to condemn. Holly just hoped and prayed that the two boys would be found quickly, safe and well.

None of them had mentioned the disused quarry beyond the woods that lay to the east of the house and gardens—in fact, they'd all carefully avoided mentioning it—but she knew it must be at the back of everyone's mind. She'd heard Ian Webster and Niall discussing the man who had died in a diving accident in the water-filled pit there, just the previous summer. It made Holly's blood run cold to think of the two boys out there all alone.

It dawned on her about ten minutes later that she'd lost her way. God, that was all they needed on top of everything else, a house guest who couldn't find her way back to her room!

Holly paused and sat down on a step while she tried to get her bearings. She peered up and down the long corridor but nothing looked familiar. She didn't feel inspired to smile as she examined the framed set of original eighteenth-century political cartoons on the wall beside her. It was as she stood there wondering what to do next that she became aware of a noise that couldn't be solely attributed to the sounds of an old house. Freezing, she strained her ears.

Could the two boys still be in the house while everyone was searching for them outside on the sprawling estate? Well what did she have to lose? If it turned out to be a noisy case of death watch beetle, who'd be the wiser? Holly set off in the direction of the faint sounds.

The sounds, which grew more distinct, led her all the way up to the attics. Seeing a dusty footprint, Holly let out a sigh of relief—it was only a little larger than her own tiny foot.

'Hello, is anyone there?' she called out robustly. It had been a while since she'd heard anything.

She was rewarded for her efforts with a very definite cry. Worryingly, the cry had sounded suspiciously like *help*!

Her stubborn efforts were rewarded when she pushed open the third attic-room door. Like the other two rooms, these high walls also showed unmistakable signs of water damage. Unlike the other rooms, scaffolding had been set up down the far end of the room and the roof plaster had been stripped back to reveal the heavy ancient wooden beams of the vaulted ceiling.

Holly didn't actually take in details of the ongoing fight against the ravages of time, her horror struck eyes were riveted on the two figures that made up the heart-stopping tableau on top of the platform fixed high up the partly erected scaffolding.

Tom was crouched down on his knees, his face red with

exertion as he held desperately onto his bigger and heavier cousin's sweatshirt, the neck of which was snagged on the top of the scaffold. The thin garment was the only thing stopping the boy plunging down to the ground; it was also in danger of throttling him. It pulled tight against his neck and Tom's valiant efforts were pulling it even tighter. Holly felt sick as she saw that these efforts might free the sweatshirt and send the boy crashing to the ground.

Holly wasn't conscious of making a decision; she was almost surprised to find herself seconds later halfway up the scaffold, shouting calm words of encouragement to the boys.

'It's fine, Tom, I'll take over,' she panted as she heaved herself over the edge of the platform.

'Pull him up, quick, he can't breathe!' The youngster released his grip as Holly took his place.

'I won't let that happen.' There was a determined set to her chin as Holly lay on her stomach—she tried not to look down, as she wasn't too good with heights—and linked her arms under Daniel's armpits. The child's breathing became immediately easier. She found it reassuring that Daniel was recovered enough to start wailing loudly over his predicament.

Holly soon realised that at this angle she wasn't going to be able to hoist the boy up over the edge of the platform. He probably weighed considerably more than she did and she just didn't have the strength in her arms. The slight amount she'd managed to raise him had been enough to unsnag the jumper, so now she was taking all his weight. Her racing mind contemplated the few options open to her. Tom sniffed, and wiped a grimy hand over his tear-stained face. 'What are you going to do now?' He sounded completely confident that she'd know the answer.

It struck Holly that the confidence of a child was a heavy

burden all on its own. 'Daniel's going to stop kicking, aren't you, sweetheart?' Another kick like the last one, and her arms were going to be wrenched out of the sockets. 'And you're going to go and get help. You can do that, can't you, Tom?'

The boy was already shinning down the scaffolding with the agility of a little monkey.

'Be careful!' she yelled out.

'I'll be back!' he called, just before she heard the door slam.

Oh, I hope so, I really hope so, she silently prayed.

'I don't like heights,' the precariously suspended boy told her in a tremulous tone.

She repressed the urge to wonder out loud why, if that were the case, he'd climbed up here in the first place! From a professional standpoint she was happy to hear that, but for a slight hoarseness, there didn't seem to be any lasting damage from his near-strangulation.

'Why don't you close your eyes?' she suggested. She did the cheerful, isn't-this-a-great-adventure note so well that anyone hearing her speak would be completely convinced she was having a ball!

By the time her grin-and-bear-it smile had turned into a grimace of pain and she knew in minute detail about every pet Daniel had ever owned—nervousness made him garrulous—the burning in the muscles of her shoulders had turned from red-hot needles of discomfort to white-hot knives of agony.

In the morning, this will all be a bad dream, she told herself, as she made the worrying discovery that even closing her eyes couldn't cut out the shoal of red dots that danced before her eyes. I can't let go, I can't let go...

She was concentrating so hard that she didn't hear the door burst open. One minute, her own laboured breathing had been the loudest thing in the room; the next, there was suddenly what seemed to be lots of people shouting. One voice seemed to separate itself from the general clamour.

'Let go, Holly. Chris will catch him.'

'I can let go?' she heard herself ask Niall stupidly. 'You're sure?'

'Absolutely.'

She did and there was a loud applause as Daniel was caught by his father. Holly, grinning foolishly, opened her eyes and looked down—mistake! Major mistake! The room spun wildly, and irrational terror froze her to the spot.

'Come on down, Holly!' she heard Thomas urge.

Holly tried to speak but nothing came out; she swallowed to lubricate her bone-dry throat.

'I can't,' she squeaked.

'Why not?' Even though her eyes were closed, she knew this was Niall.

'I don't like heights. Actually,' she confessed with a slightly wild laugh, 'I hate them!'

There was a startled pause.

'Don't you go up, Niall. You're too heavy,' Chris said. 'The whole thing looks like it could come down like pack of cards.'

I could have done without knowing that. Holly let out a faint whimper as she heard Niall snarl an angry response. She felt the metal structure vibrate as someone moved upwards. Niall never did listen to anyone. This time, Holly was glad of it.

The touch on her shoulder let her know she wasn't alone. 'I'm going to get you down.'

'It's much more likely I'll make us both fall,' she warned him. 'I'm likely to do something stupid.'

'So what's new?' he growled.

She was convinced she couldn't move, but Niall was even more convinced she could and would. He was a very good persuader, surprisingly patient, but no soft touch; he took no notice when she said she couldn't.

Her descent was painfully slow but eventually her feet were back down on terra firma. She lifted her head and Niall, who had been one rung below her all the way down, smiled. His hard mouth didn't quiver; the smile was all in his eyes, and the warmth of those eyes made her breathless condition ten times worse.

'Thank you.' Her knees were shaking so hard that she felt obliged to hold onto him to steady herself. 'I'm sorry I swore at you,' she added with a selfconscious grimace. She hadn't always appreciated his refusal to let her give up.

'I've been called worse things, but rarely with as much conviction.'

'She's saved my son's life and *she* says thank you!'

Holly's head was still spinning when Jude grabbed her and almost hugged the breath from her lungs. From scapegoat to saviour in the space of a hour was a dizzying journey to make.

'For pity's sake, Jude, let the girl breathe,' Niall rasped, impatiently detaching his sister from a very pale faced Holly.

Holly smiled her intense gratitude at him. 'I know this is feeble but I think I might be going to...'

'Did I faint?' she asked a few minutes later.

A firm hand in the middle of her chest forced her back into a prone position. 'You went down like a sack of spuds, but you probably weigh less.'

Just my luck, I didn't even get to enjoy the ride, she

thought, examining with covetous eyes the suggestion of well-formed biceps through the linen shirt he wore.

She was still feeling slightly hazy about the details of their rescue. 'The boys were all right?' She was in a sitting room she'd never been in before. By this house's standards, it had almost cosy proportions.

Niall moved his head in soothing confirmation and Holly's body sagged with relief. 'Thanks to you.' His deep voice was grim as he silently contemplated a far less pleasant outcome to the boys' disobedience. 'Hopefully they're feeling suitably chastened, just now.'

'I hope you haven't been too tough on them.' His fingers brushed her forehead and she felt them move lightly over her hair—it wasn't an entirely unpleasant sensation. In fact...'What are you doing?'

'Cobwebs,' he explained, holding up his fingers and blowing the dusty gossamer fibres from his fingers. 'You're covered in them.'

His words made her conscious of the fact she was very grubby indeed. She shot upright, looking anxiously at the chintz-covered sofa she was stretched out on.

'Will you lie down?'

'I bet you say that to all the girls.' Her lips unconsciously tightened.

'One of my best-tried lines,' he confirmed drily. 'Seriously, Holly, you ought to rest.' He regarded her face with narrow-eyed concern; habitually pale, her milky skin seemed almost transparent at that moment, but considering how little sleep she'd had last night, possibly fatigue was a contributory factor to that.

His breath quickened as his body responded spontaneously to the thought of their night together. He wanted her now, right here; the raw urgency of his need was intense enough to shock him. His eyes darkened and his throat worked as he recalled the exact raw needy note in her voice as she'd cried out in the extremity of sexual frenzy.

'Nonsense, I'm absolutely fine now. Just deeply embarrassed at being such a wimp. I've always had this thing about heights,' she explained uncomfortably.

'Which makes what you did all the more extraordinary.' His blue eyes had a fervour which was lacking in his level observation. 'Do you make a habit of saving people's lives? First the restaurant,' he reminded her. 'Now Dan.'

Holly flushed with embarrassment. There were a lot of emotions she'd like to evoke in Niall, but gratitude wasn't one of them. 'I was just in the right place,' she mumbled. 'Well, actually,' she corrected, 'I was in the wrong place—I got lost. I wasn't concentrating.' She could hardly tell him she'd been wandering around, feeling sorry for herself. 'I heard you talking about the restoration work with your father,' she recalled, feeling the grime of several centuries in her hair and grimacing. 'I should have thought. Boys that age…'

'As a father of a boy that age, *I* should have thought,' he contradicted her grimly. 'Warning the boys to keep away from the attic seems in this to have had the opposite effect. I should have remembered how appetising forbidden fruit immediately becomes,' he drawled drily. 'It's just lucky for us you have no sense of direction, and strong arms. I now know what clinging on for grim death really means. You weren't going to let go, were you…?' His words sounded more like accusation than admiration, and there was a strained expression in the burning eyes fixed on her face.

'What can I say?' She shrugged her shoulders. 'I'm stubborn.' He watched the bleakness chase across her face. 'Besides, if I hadn't stopped you leaving early this morning,' she reminded him in a small miserable voice, 'none of this would have happened.'

With a sharp exclamation of annoyance, Niall caught her chin in his hand and forced her to look up at him.

'You're filthy, Niall.' She noticed for the first time the dust ingrained like heavy theatrical make-up in the faint lines that bracketed his mouth and fanned out from the corners of his eyes. If his face had any minor imperfections, it would have highlighted them. Hungrily, her eyes skimmed lovingly over the sharply angular blemish-free contours of his strong face.

The sharp dismissive shake of his head said clearly he wasn't much interested in his personal hygiene just now. 'That's ridiculous and you know it.'

'Do I...?' She pulled her chin away and tried to ignore the fact she missed the warm contact of his strong fingers. She rotated her stiff shoulders, painfully aware that her abused muscles were already beginning to stiffen.

Niall gave an exasperated sigh. 'Jude was hitting out at anyone, earlier on; she was scared. You should have heard what she said to me before you came in. I don't need to ask permission before I make love to my fiancée at any time of day.' He looked and sounded incredulous that anyone should think otherwise.

Holly doubted Niall had asked anyone's permission for anything in years...if ever. For once, she felt surprisingly tolerant of his supreme arrogance.

'I'm not your fiancée.' She gave a breezy smile to show how well she could cope with this situation, and refused to allow the achingly wistful note to emerge.

'Yes, well, we'll talk about that later...' He obviously wasn't going to let the facts get in the way of his argument. 'Anyway,' he continued smoothly, 'as far as Jude and everyone else is concerned, you've been elevated to divine status. It's going to be very hard to dump you now without having the whole pack shrieking for my blood.'

Underneath the sardonic amusement of his smile, there was something else in his intent gaze that made her heart begin to work overtime. Now, don't go seeing something that isn't there, she crossly warned her optimistic heart.

'I could be really awful for what's left of the weekend, if you like,' she suggested helpfully. For someone as gifted as I am for saying the wrong thing, how hard could it be to turn myself into a social outcast? 'I could be so bad, they'll all breathe a sigh of relief when you dump me…Though actually, I don't much like the idea of you dumping me.'

It's not got me singing from the rooftops, either, Niall realised, looking at the threads of gold glinting through the dust on her bent head with stunned eyes.

'I'd much prefer to be the one doing the dumping, and that way nobody can blame you.'

If Niall's smile seemed a little strained, Holly didn't notice. 'That's as may be, but a man has his pride,' he announced, adopting a comically injured expression.

'Pooh,' she hooted, entering into the spirit of things. 'Being dumped by your fiancée is not nearly so bad as being dumped by your wife, and you've…' Her hand went immediately to her open mouth. 'Oh, God,' she babbled, 'I didn't mean to make it sound as if—'

'Being dumped by your wife is not a pride-enhancing experience,' he admitted frankly, regarding her horror-struck expression with amusement. 'But I'm not so emotionally fragile that you have to walk on eggshells. It all happened a long time ago.'

Holly remained gloomily unconvinced. If you loved someone, time didn't enter into the equation—she of all people should know that—and he would say that, wouldn't he…? He wasn't the type to parade his emotional scars.

'Tara copes well in a crisis.'

'A lot of people make the mistake of thinking she's an airhead,' Niall responded drily.

'Well, I'm not one of them,' she snapped, very conscious of how swiftly he'd flown to Tara's defence. 'You still care for her a lot, don't you?' she persisted masochistically.

'We've shared a lot together…'

Holly smiled thinly. Well, she hadn't really expected him to deny a bond that was so patently obvious.

'I'll always love, Tara…'

Holly closed her eyes.

Serves me right for asking, she thought.

'But I'm not in love with her any more,' he added softly.

Holly's eyes shot open. *'Really?'* Hearing the eagerness in her voice, she felt a warm rush of hot colour wash over her fair skin. 'You don't have to tell me this.'

'Pity…'

A wary frown puckered her smooth brow. 'Is it?'

'I was kind of hoping that you're not an entirely disinterested party?' There was a disturbing smile as he waited for her response.

His words might just have the potential to put a new and remarkable spin on things. If her brain hadn't stopped functioning, she'd probably have been able to figure out what that spin might be.

'Why should it matter to me if you're in love or not with Tara?'

'It might affect your decision to carry on seeing me.'

Holly clenched her feebly fluttering hands to her sides. She swallowed and tried to sound casual. 'Seeing you? After this weekend, you mean?'

'You sound shocked. Surely it isn't such an extraordinary idea, after last night? Or are you saying that nights like that come along every day of the week for you?' There was frustration mingled with the glint of dry humour in his eyes.

'No,' she denied readily. 'But I thought maybe they did for you.'

Niall's shrewd glance narrowed. Unless Holly had a sex life that defied belief, what she'd said betrayed a surprising naiveté that inclined him to rethink quite a lot of things. Maybe she had seemed to act as if she'd never done certain things before because she hadn't…A disbelieving laugh was wrenched from him, but his expression was sober enough as it locked with hers—in fact, it was deadly earnest.

'They don't.'

Her mind was racing. Did that mean he'd thought it was special? How special? She waited with breathless impatience for him to fill in the infuriating gaps left by his terse response.

'Last night…' It was strange to see the articulate Niall almost fumble for words to describe what they'd shared. 'Was not like any other I've spent,' he rasped. 'You were incredible…Last night was incredible, this morning was incredible, and, call me crazy, but I don't see any reason not to repeat the experience on a regular basis. If I were a pessimist, I'd say the only way to go after sex like that was down.' Niall's nostrils flared as he took a deep breath. He sought and captured her eyes.

Holly was stunned by his admissions. The challenging smile that curved his amazing sensual lips made her start shaking feverishly.

'But I'm prepared to risk it if you are,' he admitted in

a deep sexy drawl that sent a plump voluptuous shiver dripping down her spine.

It was pretty satisfying to have it confirmed by a second party—second *interested* party—that last night hadn't been ordinary. And Niall should know, she told herself; he did have a lot more room for comparison than she did!

'How will that work? I mean, I know you're not asking me to marry you.' Her laugh invited him to share the joke—he didn't. 'Which,' she added soberly, 'is just as well, because marriage isn't on my agenda for years and years—not until I'm established in my career.' Her fierce frown defied him to argue the point—he didn't.

'I think you've mentioned that point before…'

There was no harm reinforcing it. 'Marriage is only one possibility for a woman,' she told him earnestly. 'People assume…'

'People being men.'

Holly gritted her teeth determined to show him she could match anyone in the cynicism stakes. 'People assume that every woman wants marriage and babies…'

'Is this a direct Rowena quote?' he enquired with interest. 'If I hadn't seen how happy your parents are with my own eyes, I'd have assumed you're both the products of a particularly bitter divorce.'

'I'm not some Rowena clone!' she shrieked.

'I already know that,' came the dry response. 'If I promise not to propose.' His heavy ironic tone made her feel gauche and clumsy. 'We could see one another, go out occasionally…' The hot look he shot her made Holly's stomach dissolve into an erotic black hole 'And stay in a lot.'

His message came through loud and clear. He wasn't talking exploring a deep mutual bond, here; he wasn't talking love—he was talking *sex*! And where will I be when the novelty wears off? she asked herself. Still fathoms in love, that's where, you idiot. Cut your losses now: you're only delaying the inevitable, the sane voice of logic in her head told her sternly.

'I'm starting my stint on paeds—paediatrics—next month. I'll be working long hours…' As excuses went, this one was just begging to be demolished. You could have at least *pretended* to think about saying no, she told herself with self-disgust.

'All the more need for relaxation.' His relaxed expression suggested that there never was any question over her reply.

'I'm a bit of a couch potato when I finally do get any time off,' she warned him. 'Not very entertaining company.'

'I'm sold by all these lures you're throwing in my direction.' There was a thread of steel in his sardonic tone. 'Be careful, Holly, or I might get the idea you're not keen.'

'For heaven's sake!' she snapped. 'You know perfectly well I'm keen.' She blushed deeply—considering some of the things she'd babbled at him in the grip of mindless passion, he must be aware that *keen* didn't begin to cover the way she felt about him. 'I wish I wasn't!' There was no mistaking the heartfelt sincerity of this statement.

'Is it the idea of the baggage I carry around that worries you?' Niall speculated in a hard, cynical voice. 'Is this another of your lifestyle choices: you don't date fathers?'

'You're my first.' First love, last love, she thought, feeling the warmth of unshed tears fill her eyes. She turned her head away and blinked rapidly to clear the suspect moisture. 'But that's more by luck than good judgment.'

'It looks like your luck has run out.' His dark, fierce face came very close to hers as he drew a line through the chalky grime on her cheek with the tip of his forefinger.

'I don't mind.' Twisting her fingers into his hair, she made the husky confession almost defiantly. God, she needed him any way she could have him. She'd show him she could be as casual as him if it killed her!

His electric blue eyes smouldered with triumph as he swept her into his powerful arms. 'I think we're going to have a lot of fun,' he told her, just before he nuzzled the delicate area beside her ear.

Holly was all for fun, but it didn't suggest depth of commitment. Was it so wrong to want those things? she wondered bleakly. She firmly buried her restless sense of dissatisfaction as Niall chose that moment to torment her lips with a series of soft muted kisses.

He laughed deep in his throat when she growled softly and tightened her grip on his hair. 'Is this what you want?'

The kiss drove the air from her lungs and left her wanting more—much more!

Her lips moved to form a sultry smile. 'You're on the right track.'

'Well, was it so bad?' Niall asked as his wildly waving family diminished from view in the rear window.

'I had a nice time, thank you.' Holly looked at her hands neatly folded in her lap rather than at the man beside her. It was one thing to play the fiancée for an audience; it was quite another to act the girlfriend...

'Even after Mum's attempts to teach you to ride.' Niall didn't seem to share her feelings of awkwardness.

'You can laugh!' She raised indignant eyes to his amused face. 'But you wouldn't be,' she added darkly, 'if you had to sit on my—'

'If you're going to do anything as stupid as fall off a pony, it's the best place to land.' Niall was looking towards the area where her 'best place' was cushioned by blissfully soft upholstery.

'It wasn't a pony, it was a horse.' A great stomping thing at least ten feet tall!

'I thought, by the way you were looking at it, it might have been a fire-breathing dragon.'

Holly's lips twitched. 'I'm never getting on a horse again.'

'Quitter,' Niall taunted. He glanced over his shoulder into the back seat, where his son was already nodding off. 'They can smell the fear…so can I.' The swift sideways look he shot her was not nearly so casual as his sly dig.

Holly looked stubbornly at the road ahead and tried to brazen it out. Her brow furrowed in innocent incomprehension. She silently cursed his damned uncanny perception.

'I won't throw you if you mount me,' he promised helpfully.

'*Niall!*' she remonstrated, hot-cheeked. She glanced furtively towards the back seat. Tom, who'd spent the morning playing a rough game of soccer with the menfolk, was already sound asleep.

'I'm only trying to put you at your ease,' he protested mildly.

'Then I have to tell you you've failed,' she croaked, trying to get all those lurid images of her astride…No she wouldn't think about it!

'Tell me what's wrong, Holly,' he persisted. 'And don't bother denying it. You haven't insulted me for at least half an hour, so I know something's got you worried.'

'I'm not worried. It's just this is all a bit unexpected. Circumstances have made things happen rather quickly. The couple thing…I mean…this…us…'

'Are you trying to tell me you're not the sort of girl who sleeps with the guy on the first date?'

'I know you're a good driver,' she said, as his fingers curled around her thigh. The pressure they exerted was rather nice, actually. A small choking sound escaped her throat as she felt her nipples harden instantly. 'But I'd prefer you kept both hands on the wheel.' Her sigh of relief when he complied had less to do with fear for their physical safety and more to do with fear for her sanity. 'We've not even had a date yet,' she reminded him shrilly.

'We can fix that. I'm taking Tom ice-skating tomorrow. We go most weeks. Come with us.'

'Most weeks: does that mean you're good at it?' she wondered suspiciously.

'I get by.'

What the hell? He'd already seen her fall off a horse; there wasn't as far to fall on skates. 'All right. Won't Tom mind…? I mean, I don't want to intrude on your private time with him. He might resent it.'

'Tom thinks you're cool.'

'I like him, too,' she admitted gruffly.

'You've not had a lot of boyfriends, have you, Holly?' he asked gently.

'Nothing intense.' Meaning I'm feeling pretty intense now—nicely done, Holly, she chided herself. There was no way Niall could have missed that. Rather to her surprise, he didn't push her farther. 'This is a bit of turnaround, considering what you thought of me at first…'

He winced. 'I thought you'd forgotten that.'

'I never forget anything,' she boasted firmly.

'*Nothing?* You're starting to scare me,' he told her drily.

'Maybe you should be.' Her brow puckered.

He sighed. 'We're talking adolescent trauma here, aren't

we? That night I chucked out your would-be lover? Perhaps we should get this out in the open.'

His perception once more was uncannily accurate. 'Actually, he ran without any encouragement, Niall.'

'Probably just as well. I wasn't feeling very kindly disposed towards...Well, anyone, actually...including myself.'

'It wasn't just me, then? I suppose that makes me feel better.' She wrinkled her nose dubiously.

'I can still remember that hurt puppy expression in your eyes. I felt like a total bastard.'

'You *were* a total bastard.'

'Though it was easier to live with my conscience after you'd kicked me.' He shuddered, and let his eyes momentarily rest on the moody quiver of her generous lower lip. 'Jude had just told me she was pregnant and her precious bloody Richard still had a wife.' The words came out quickly and his discomfort in revealing this to her was pretty obvious. 'I think I'd run out of understanding, especially for young women bent on self-destruction.'

'I wasn't—' she began to protest, only to be impatiently interrupted.

'Just put semantics to one side, for once. I know you were a kid...'

Holly bit her lip and let his grouchiness pass. She'd actually been going to contest the self-destructive part of his statement.

'Jude wanted me to explain to Mum and Dad that everything would be all right eventually because he was going to leave his wife when the time was right...*Can you believe it?*' The memory still had the power now to turn his knuckles white against the steering wheel. 'As you can imagine, I was looking forward no end to that conversation. If I hadn't been so bloody wrapped up in my own life, I might have been there to protect her...' He made a sound of disgust in his throat and stared grimly at the road ahead. 'I don't suppose she'd have listened to me.'

With understanding came a surge of compassion for Niall—who had blamed himself for not being there when his sister needed him—and Jude. Poor Jude: you couldn't compare an inexperienced teenage grope with what had happened to her, but Niall, frustrated by his inability to help his sister, had obviously seen a tenuous parallel.

'She probably wouldn't have,' she agreed, sliding her hand between her knee and the leather upholstery, because the urge to reach out and physically comfort him was getting awfully hard to resist. 'We don't listen when we think we're in love.'

'Are you speaking from experience?'

It wasn't until he spoke that she realised how her thoughtless words might be interpreted. 'What sort of question is that to ask?' she responded indignantly. 'Do I go asking you details about your love life?'

'Whether you ask or not, you seem to know one hell of a lot. Actually I wasn't really thinking about the past...'

Holly went pale. 'You're asking me if I'm in love with you?' she squeaked.

'Possibly...In a subtle, roundabout way.'

'Don't worry.' She managed a passably jaunty grin. 'I won't subject you to repeat performance of heavy sighs and soulful stares.' She swallowed the taste of bile in her throat.

Talking about the dim and distant past, when she'd dogged his every step, had obviously aroused memories of her embarrassingly obvious devotion. The idea of a repetition was obviously filling Niall with alarm. It was the only reason she could imagine for the sudden inquisition. Niall didn't want any complications in their relationship—like love. She was going to have to be more cautious in the future.

'I'm relieved.'

Holly suspected she hadn't quite convinced him. She put her all into her breezy response.

'You won't need to send out the heavy mob to get the ring back, either.' She slid the ring off her finger and solemnly held it out to him. She thought for a moment that he was going to refuse it.

'It suited you,' he said almost absently as he dropped the gem into his breast pocket.

'It made me nervous, walking around with a small fortune on my finger,' she told him hoarsely.

'I don't think it was the market value that was bothering you.'

Holly didn't want to go down that road. She smiled brightly. 'I'd like to invite you in when we get back, but…'

'I'd like to come in…but…' Niall too looked at his sleeping son.

They both left it at that, but Holly was aware this was a subject which wasn't going to go away. She couldn't hide what she felt forever. Love was a hindrance, from Niall's point of view, to the sort of adult, no-strings-attached relationship he wanted.

CHAPTER EIGHT

'Wow, when did you learn to cook?' Rowena sniffed appreciatively and dumped her overnight bag on the floor.

Jaw ajar, spoon in hand, a startled Holly whirled around. 'What are you doing here?' She blew the rebellious bright strands of hair out of her eyes and realised her response had sounded perilously like an accusation.

'I live here—remember?' One artistically plucked eyebrow rose towards her sister's stylish hairline.

The mild mockery only increased Holly's hot-cheeked dismay. 'I wasn't expecting—you took me by surprise,' she babbled, trying to compensate for her lukewarm welcome with an extra bright smile. 'Great to see you.' Why did Rowena have to turn up now, of all times, looking so disgustingly *perfect*. Unfortunately her tone showed a tendency to echo her lack of enthusiasm.

Stifling a childish urge to push her sister back out of the door—if only the Rowena complication could be solved that easily—Holly put her spoon down before she hugged Rowena. 'I like your new haircut.'

That at least was true. The soft style disguised but didn't completely hide the fact that her sister had lost some weight. Rowena was still stunning, of course, in a new toned, lean, hungry—I work out twice a day—sort of way.

'You should try a new look yourself, Holly. You'd be amazed at how much difference it could make.'

Holly didn't take offence to the obvious implication that her old look needed a bit of work; it was true, especially

134

at the moment when the steamy atmosphere in the kitchen
had made her once-smooth chignon frizz around the edges.

'Actually,' Rowena continued slowly, surveying her sister from shrewd china-blue eyes, 'you *do* look different.
It's not the hair…Speaking of which, I know a really good
hairdresser who…All right.' She gave a concessionary
shrug. 'Just promise me you'll never again try and cut your
fringe yourself.'

'That was years ago. I couldn't afford to go to the hairdresser's then.'

'You still couldn't afford to go to a decent hairdresser.'
Rowena had been appalled to discover what her sister's
salary was after so many years' study. 'Talking money,
how would you feel about a little monthly column when I
come back: women and health, that sort of thing? It would
be for a trial period to begin with, of course, but it's the
sort of thing that would take off, I'm sure.'

'*Me*, write?' Holly said blankly.

'If you can't, I'll sack you. Nepotism is all right, so long
as it's good business. It pays.'

Rowena mentioned a sum that made Holly's knees go
weak.

'Think about it,' Rowena advised. 'There really is something different about you. What…?'

Her words only confirmed something Holly had puzzled
over when looking in the mirror earlier; they also sent
alarm bells ringing in her head. It was only a matter of
time before Rowena cottoned on the fact it wasn't what,
but *who* that had brought about these subtle alterations in
her own appearance. True, she'd not been transformed
overnight into a raving beauty, and to say she had an inner
radiance would have been wildly over the top, not to mention soppy: but there was something indefinably different.

'Is anything wrong? What brings you back?' Holly put

a lot of effort into sounding interested. She glanced nervously at the clock—oh, no! He'd be here any minute.

Rowena's slender shoulders lifted as she shrugged off the beautifully cut linen jacket she wore over a plain black T-shirt and the sort of snug-fitting leather jeans that only one woman in fifty looked half-decent in—Rowena looked sensational. 'Impulse.' She didn't quite meet her sister's eyes. 'I had a free weekend so I thought I'd see if you had remembered to feed the fish.'

Panic-stricken, Holly looked around the room, half-expecting to see some unfortunate creatures floating glassy-eyed and neglected in a tank. 'Fish! You don't…Do you…?'

'No, Holly, I don't; it was a joke, darling.' She lifted the heavy strands of ash-blonde hair off the nape of her neck before she dropped gracefully into a deeply padded swivel chair.

Holly saw Rowena's slow smile—the one that fascinated every man she'd ever met—appear as she rested her chin on the bridge of her interlocked fingers. Holly loved her sister dearly but she often wished Rowena wasn't so fascinatingly beautiful.

'It's a man, isn't it?' Rowena gave a delighted crow of laughter as Holly squirmed uncomfortably. 'I knew it! It must be serious if you've learnt to cook.'

Holly grimaced reproachfully at this reference to her culinary skills. During a brief flirtation with domesticity during her teens, the local birdlife had been the best-fed—although the *best* part had been hotly disputed—in the area. Famously, *nothing* Holly produced in the kitchen had ever made it as far as the table.

'I've not learnt,' she admitted, eyeing the cookbook from hell with loathing. 'I'm learning and, if you must know, surprise, surprise, it's a total disaster!' She pressed a harassed hand to her sticky forehead. It hadn't taken her long to realise that she'd been far too ambitious attempting the Thai dish. I ought to have bought Marks and Spencers ready-prepared and lied, she thought.

'Careful!' Rowena cried, leaping gracefully to her feet. 'Are those chillies on your fingers? Don't go near your eyes.'

Holly automatically snatched her hands away from her face and extended them gloomily. 'I've lost count of the things I've chopped—including my fingers. I think I've made a wise decision, not opting for surgery.'

'Go wash your hands,' Rowena insisted, elbowing her away from the work counter. She glanced at the recipe and then looked at the cover of the book Holly was using. 'I've used this one; it's quite simple.' She tucked her pale hair behind her ears in a businesslike fashion.

'No, Rowena, really, it's fine. You must be jet-lagged—we'll eat out.'

'I flew Concorde,' Rowena announced with a mellow smile, 'and cooking relaxes me. It *does*,' she insisted, in reply to Holly's scathing hoot of derision. 'Besides, I want to hear all about this man of yours.'

Holly awkwardly avoided her sister's curious gaze. They'd never had any cosy girlie chats about boyfriends over the years. She wasn't sure whether, under the circumstances, now was the best time to start.

Considering Rowena's long-standing and more importantly *unspecific* relationship with Niall, Holly felt distinctly uneasy about admitting to her sister that he was the new man in her life. It was almost as if saying it out loud would make her realise how foolish the idea was. She was also aware of the deep streak of possessiveness in her sister's nature. Rowena had never been very forgiving if her little sister had messed with her things. She wasn't pathological or anything, but…!

'He's not mine,' Holly insisted awkwardly. Admitting it brought a bleak droop to her soft lips.

She perched on a stool and watched Rowena calmly creating order out of her chaos. It was amazing enough to be able to cook without so much as glancing at the endless list of exotic ingredients in the glossy cookery book, but to be able to do that and look like an ice princess was nothing short of miraculous in Holly's book.

'Do you do *anything* badly?' she burst out with rueful affection.

Rowena's laugh was bitter. 'Where should I start? How about relationships…?'

Holly was amazed by this revealing remark. 'Is something wrong, Rowena?…Ouch!' She winced as she eased herself off the stool.

'What's wrong?'

Holly rubbed her tender rear. 'I went ice-skating this morning…I spent all the time I wasn't crawling on all fours on my backside,' she admitted ruefully. 'And I fell off a horse down at Monksleigh.'

'I forgot you went there. Isn't it a dreamy place? I could get used to the life of the landed gentry.'

'I thought they were pretty down-to-earth,' Holly suggested tentatively.

'Yeah, I suppose they are. Tell me, was Miss Beautiful-but-dim there? Tara?' she elaborated impatiently.

Holly nodded. 'She's not dim.'

'No, but she is beautiful, so permit me a bit of green-eyed monster.'

Holly was amazed by the notion that her sister could envy any woman's looks. Or perhaps the envy was directed more at the fact Tara had been married to Niall.

Rowena's next words seemed to confirm the latter might well be true.

'I never thought she was the right woman for Niall.' Rowena looked grimly pleased that time had proved her right. 'I tried to warn him, but he wouldn't listen.'

'And you *expected* him to?'

'Ouch! That sounds pretty bitter. Would I be wrong to assume Niall has been winding you up?' She laughed. 'The bad man. I'll have words with him when I see him. The least he could do under the circumstances was be nice to you.'

Holly swallowed. 'Actually, he was *quite* nice...Mostly,' she admitted diffidently.

Rowena's face cleared. 'I should hope so too. 'Though I can't imagine what possessed you to get on a horse, even for him. I know how persuasive he can be, but...' The secret smile made Holly feel nauseous. 'Now, skates I *don't* understand. You've never had any sense of balance...Did you ever finally get rid of the stabilisers on your bike?'

'After a fashion.'

'Good God, was this a *date* today with your new man?' From Rowena's expression, it was pretty obvious that ice-skating wasn't her idea of romance. 'I suppose,' she conceded, 'there are romantic possibilities attached to slithering into the right set of arms.'

'His son was there.'

Holly had done a lot of slithering and Niall had been there to catch her once or twice. Heat crawled over her skin as she recalled how it had felt on the occasions he'd felt obliged to clasp her unsteady figure protectively against his body—probably more often than was strictly necessary, if truth be told. Holly had felt no reason to complain at the time—she still didn't.

'He's married?'

'Divorced.'

'Are you sure about that?' Rowena enquired cynically.

'Quite sure…Actually, Rowena he's—'

Rowena gave a thin-lipped cynical smile and waved her hand. 'Absolutely perfect, I'm sure,' she sneered. 'I suppose that's him now.'

Holly nodded as the door bell pealed insistently. 'Probably.'

'Well, aren't you going to answer it?'

Holly fumbled with the lock and wondered why she hadn't just come straight out and told Rowena. It wasn't as if she was doing anything wrong. Why the hell do I feel so guilty? she wondered.

Niall, a bottle of wine clasped in one hand, stepped over the threshold. His expression as his eyes lighted on Holly gave a very flattering impression of raw hunger.

Holly's stomach-muscles clenched painfully, she felt weakly light-headed as a hot tide of desire rushed over her. As always, he looked incredible. How did he manage to do this to her, just standing there? In that second of breathless admiration and growing anticipation, she forgot all about Rowena and her disapproval.

'Niall,' she breathed huskily.

'Niall?' Rowena echoed, abandoning her steaming wok. 'It is you!' she exclaimed joyously as she flew straight past Holly, who automatically stepped back—she'd had a lot of practice stepping back for Rowena. 'How did you know I was back? Did you get the message I left with your service?' she asked, throwing her arms around his neck and planting a warm kiss on his lips.

The sound of Rowena's voice had broken the spell for Holly, who was pierced by a stab of white-hot jealousy as she saw Niall's free hand go automatically around Rowena's slender waist.

They made a stunning pair. She masochistically forced herself to study the artistically pleasing picture they made as Niall returned the kiss with equally unselfconscious enthusiasm. The concerns Holly had almost successfully pushed to the back of her mind since they'd become lovers came rushing back. Were he and Rowena really just *good friends*? Rowena never flaunted her relationships and where her private life was concerned she was never very forthcoming.

Just when Holly had begun to darkly wonder whether they were going in for some sort of endurance record, they broke apart, although her sister's hand did stay on the lapel of the black leather jacket he wore.

'I didn't know you were back.'

'Then why this?' Rowena pressed, taking the bottle from his hand. She surveyed the label and let out an appreciative whistle. 'Not that I'm complaining. You can entertain me while little sister here is busy with her new man.' She turned her teasing stare on Holly. 'You've seen more of her recently than me, Niall.'

The satiric glitter in his eyes was too much for Holly's composure. She sent him a reproachful look of wild appeal and began to choke noisily.

'I told you to wash the chillies off, Holly.' Rowena spared her a second before turning her full attention back to Niall. 'You never did say: did your family swallow the girlfriend story? I must say, I had my doubts. You must tell me *everything* later. Right now, I want to know about this divorced man. Has Holly 'fessed up to you, Niall? She's gone all mysterious on me. Do you know who he is…?'

Rowena saw his eyes move very obviously to her sis-

ter's face. Holly, her smooth cheeks very pink, was looking pretty miserable. Perhaps she'd taken the teasing too
far…

'As matter of fact, I do.'

The possessive rasp of his deep voice had Rowena spinning back to him, an expression of burgeoning disbelief in
her blue eyes. Then she saw the way he was looking at
her sister…*Holly…?*

Slack-jawed, she did a double- and treble-take. There
was nothing very unambiguous about Niall's expression;
in fact, in some quarters it might be considered indecently
explicit, but Rowena still couldn't take it in.

When Holly had dressed earlier, choosing a short silky
black skirt and simple cowl-neck matching top, her way-
ward imagination had wilfully supplied a picture of Niall
sliding his hand under her skirt. She'd thought those erotic
images had been pretty hot, not to mention fatally distracting, yet unbelievably what she felt now simply hearing his
voice in the flesh did more for her than any steamy images
could.

There was nothing very subtle about what was happening to her. Holly was virtually immobilised with lust. She
gave a small soundless gasp and felt the muscles of her
flat stomach suck in helplessly as instant desire ripped
through her. If he'd chosen this moment to explore in a
way similar to that which she'd imagined earlier, it would
take him about two seconds flat to discover she was just
about dying for his touch!

'You and Holly? You've been…? You're…?' Rowena's
attractive voice emerged as a disbelieving croak before her
attitude turned rapidly to denial. 'No…No, that can't be
right.' She laughed.

It was the laughter that finally drew Holly's attention
back to her sister. *Yes!* she wanted to yell. *Yes*, we have

been and with any luck we're going to again—although
the way tonight was panning out didn't make that likely.
Rowena looked pale and seriously shocked by their reve-
lations, but all Holly was conscious of was the laughter.
It was a joke. That would be right…Suddenly, she was
very tired of being the light relief.

'Why not?' Giving an imperious little chin-tilt, she was
conscious that Niall had taken hold of her hand. Was the
steady pressure of his warm fingers meant to pacify or
support? Either way, Holly had stepped back for Rowena
for the last time!

A flustered Rowena tore her eyes from the image of
Niall's fingers curling around Holly's small hand. She
struggled visibly to recover her sophisticated composure.

'No offence intended.'

'None taken.' Holly's spiky tone matched her sister's in
the insincerity stakes.

'You took me by surprise, that's all. I think it's marvellous.'

Overcompensating, Holly decided stubbornly, unconvinced by Rowena's attempts at reconciliation.

'Tell me all about it…How did you two…?' Holly knew
Rowena didn't have a coy bone in her body, but to see
her looking up at Niall you'd never have guessed it.

Despite her slick recovery, Holly instinctively knew
Rowena minded. The question was, how much did she
mind and what was she going to do about it? Holly looked
worriedly at her sister, all stylish blonde hair and long,
long legs covered in soft supple leather. The sliver of flat
tanned midriff gave a glimpse of the perfection of her ce-
lestial body. If Rowena decided to retrieve her property,
what chance would Holly have?

Deep down she knew, and was guiltily distressed by the
knowledge, that she was behaving and thinking like a jeal-

ous witch. She'd been in Rowena's shadow all her life but never until this moment had she felt so bitterly resentful of the fact—not even in her angst-ridden teens!

It wasn't Rowena's fault she was beautiful and desirable and it wasn't her fault loving Niall was making Holly feel more vulnerable than ever before in her life. If he loved me back, things would be very different, Holly acknowledged, feeling the bleak taut band across her chest tighten.

'You know me...I've always been a tad territorial,' Rowena was confessing with attractive self-mockery to Niall.

Perhaps I am being paranoid, Holly thought, watching Niall respond warmly to her sister's friendly overtures. There is such a thing as platonic friendship, although in my experience men found it a lot easier to be platonic with women who look like me rather than women who looked like Rowena!

'I come back expecting to find everything the way I left it and bam! My flat, my sister, my best friend...! I'm dizzy! I've heard of while the cat is away, but this...'

'You've still got your sister.' Niall looked in her direction and Holly forced her stiff lips into a suitably harmonious grin. 'And your flat, and I'm definitely still your best friend.'

Call me old-fashioned and idealistic, Holly thought, still smiling like an idiot on the outside but feeling bleakly disillusioned inside, but wouldn't it be nice if your lover was your best friend?

With misty eyes, Rowena looked even more beautiful. 'Why, thank you, darling,' she said huskily, letting her fingers trail over his lean cheek. Holly swallowed and resisted the strong desire to slap her sister's hand away. Holly closed her eyes, willing the feeling to pass; she knew his cheek, even though he looked freshly shaven, would have that slightly abrasive quality she loved.

'Let me make dinner for you both and we can catch up.'

'It looks to me like you already were,' Niall remarked drily, glancing towards the kitchen.

'I'm a lousy cook,' Holly said as the sinking sensation in her stomach hit rock bottom. 'Rowena arrived just as I was about to throw in the spoon and suggest we eat out.'

Niall seemed deaf to the silent pleas she was broadcasting. Perhaps, she pondered resentfully, he actually *wanted* to spend a cosy night in with Rowena. He sure as hell wasn't doing much to stop things heading in that direction!

'Then isn't it lucky I arrived when I did?' Rowena started swishing around the kitchen area with teeth-clenching efficiency.

It was bad enough Rowena had been given double portions in the brains and beauty department; to make her a great cook too was adding insult to injury! Things couldn't get much worse, Holly thought, left with no alternative but to grin and bear it—predictably, they did! The evening was a nightmare!

Rowena probably didn't mean to exclude her from the conversation by introducing topics and people Holly didn't know—but then again, with Rowena, who seemed to be in dazzling form, if a bit brittle tonight, you never could tell. As the night wore on, Holly said less and less and her sister—and, more importantly, her lover—after a couple of feeble efforts to include her in the conversation, didn't seem to care less.

'You seemed a bit preoccupied tonight, Holly.' Niall had one hand braced on the wall beside the lift.

I'm surprised you noticed, Holly thought, as her simmering resentment began to boil.

'Did I? The lift's arrived.' She gestured coldly towards

the closed door of the lift, which had swished obediently up to the top floor.

'I was being polite, actually. It looked as if you were sulking.'

She spun around, an expression of indignant outrage on her face. *'Sulking?'*

'You acted deaf every time Rowena spoke to you.'

Niall couldn't recall having a more frustrating evening in his entire life and Holly had taken it into her head to go out of her way to make it even worse! Didn't she realise he'd had a hard time himself trying to act normal—and he'd made a pretty pitiful job of that—when all he'd actually wanted to do was strip off that sexy little black outfit and make love to her? He still wanted her now, after she'd displayed all the seductive qualities of a spoilt brat!

And not listening to Rowena was the height of bad taste, Holly thought belligerently. The slug of brandy she'd recklessly swigged back after dinner still glowed in her belly; it made her courageous and slightly reckless.

'Nobody could accuse *you* of not listening to her.'

'No…?' Voice smooth as silk, Niall's eyes had narrowed on her averted face.

'You hung on her every word,' she accused unimaginatively. 'Have you slept with her, Niall?' The anguished words emerged with all the subtlety of a hand grenade. Barely stifling a groan, Holly knew her skin tones had achieved a sense of oneness with her fiery hair.

'Is that what this is all about?' he grated incredulously. He took her softly rounded chin in his hand. 'Look at me, Holly.' She twisted her head away and a low growl of annoyance emerged from his throat. 'I could shake you.' Not straight away, though; there were other more immediate priorities. He swallowed convulsively as a tide of warm blood deepened his naturally dark colour by several shades.

'What an excellent basis for a relationship,' she hissed ironically. 'And I use the term loosely.'

'Are you going to go into this Cinderella routine every time Rowena walks into a room?' he demanded impatiently. 'I think it's time you learnt to deal with your insecurities; they're not attractive.'

Holly's temper spiked at this brutal afterthought. She viciously bit her trembling lower lip—he wouldn't make her cry! I suppose this is his way of telling me I'm not attractive, either, she thought.

'The way I recall it, Cinderella had two ugly sisters; I have one beautiful one.'

'Sure, Rowena's a stunner, but that doesn't mean you've any need to be jealous.'

'Tara was jealous,' she taunted him. 'And anyway, I'm not jealous as such,' she lied with cool dignity. 'How was I supposed to contribute to a conversation that concerned cute little things that happened when I was still in school?'

Niall gave a deeply exasperated sigh. 'You're acting as though you're still in school,' he told her scornfully. 'Rowena and I, we're just friends: and as her friend I couldn't help but notice she had something on her mind tonight, and I'm not just talking about me sleeping with her little sister—she was bound to be protective about that,' he mused thoughtfully. 'Rowena didn't want to be alone tonight. Surely you could see that?' he asked incredulously. 'Or were you too busy feeling sorry for yourself because you didn't have centre stage?'

Uneasily, Holly recalled briefly receiving the self-same impression of Rowena's unhappiness earlier that evening.

'Perhaps *you* should have stayed, then.' Despairingly, she heard another in the long line of childish and unattractive hackneyed responses that seemed ready to gush from her lips tonight. 'To be a supportive friend.'

Bizarrely, for someone who was sick to the stomach with fear of losing him, she seemed to be doing her level best to push Niall away.

'Do you think I like this any more than you do?' Niall snarled, suddenly taking her by the shoulders.

Drawn into a dizzyingly close proximity to his lean, taut, virile body, Holly blinked up at him, bewildered by the strained intensity in his voice. For the first time, she was conscious of a coiled tension in his strung-out body. Even as her own wretched body responded to the gratifying glitter of sexual frustration in his deep-set eyes, Holly despised her weakness.

'I've been thinking about spending tonight with you ever since we parted this afternoon—before that, even,' he confessed rawly, his eyes ranging hungrily over her face. 'If you must know, I've been counting the minutes like some silly adolescent because, to be quite frank, you're driving me ever so slightly crazy.' A strained grin cracked his taut features. 'At least you falling on the ice gave me a legitimate excuse to dust down that delightful bottom of yours.' His hands slipped to her behind as he spoke and he pulled her hard against him.

This unexpected lustful reference to her rear, closely followed by close contact with the core of a pulsing frustration he wasn't attempting to disguise, made Holly sigh in relieved delight. Her jealousies seemed suddenly irrational; they melted away, leaving her feeling foolish and embarrassed.

'Me, too,' she echoed in a husky voice. 'Counting the minutes, that is. Seeing you and Rowena together, looking so disgustingly perfect—the pair of you look like an advert to promote eugenics!'

'I know I'm in danger of sounding trivial, Holly, but I'm not interested in your genes, angel.' His smouldering restless glance gave a lot of clues about what he was interested in. 'Holly.' Huskily, he murmured her name before his tongue thrust skilfully between her slightly parted lips. There was raw desperation in the greedy erotic exploration that left her gasping noisily for breath.

'Why didn't you kiss me before?' she moaned angrily, her body stretching in a tight arc as she reached up and tightened her grip on his thick lush hair. 'I wanted you to do that so much!'

Niall felt the blood pounding in his temples when, as she drew up onto tiptoe, the rounded contours of her small firm bottom tightened deliciously under his hands. The air-conditioned atmosphere of the hallway felt more like a steamy tropical night to him as, with a muffled exclamation he thrust his hand up under her skirt, until there was only thin lace separating his fingers from her warm smooth flesh. The idea of letting his fingers wander towards that hot, silkily damp area between her legs—knowing it was what she wanted—was driving him to the edge. He was having a hard time remembering where they were.

'Starting's easy.' The tip of his tongue traced the full outline of her lower lip. 'It's stopping I have the problem with,' he groaned.

'So don't stop,' she commanded, fiercely reckless. Her hot hungry eyes fused with his.

'I don't know what the hell you've done to me.' Continually fascinated by the full plush contours of her soft pink mouth, his tongue flickered greedily out once more. The nightcap he'd sensibly refused couldn't have intoxicated him half as much as her brandy-tinged lips, he reflected grimly. 'I think I was right: you must be a witch,' he rasped.

He was seriously spellbound—or, rather, lustbound; that much was indisputable. Concentrating on what Rowena was saying tonight had been hellishly difficult and, he feared, embarrassingly obvious. Considering his friend's obvious distress, he felt all kinds of a heel.

Holly was mesmerised by his raw sensual appraisal. The shivery hot sensations that writhed in the pit of her belly had spread until her entire body was shaken by feverish little tremors. Her toes trailed uselessly on the densely carpeted floor as he took the couple of steps that had her spine hard against the wall.

The breath whooshed from her lungs as, simultaneously, every nerve fibre in her body jerked to attention. Her bones melted and submission swept through her body as she felt the imprint of his erection grinding boldly into her belly.

'Niall…!' Plea, surrender: her voice carried both these things plus a measure of the agony she saw etched on his own dark, drawn features.

He released his grip on her hips and took a step backwards. 'Sorry.' Stiffly, he drew an unsteady hand through his thick tousled hair. 'Got a bit carried away,' he added tersely.

Holly pressed the back of her hand to her trembling lips. He'd carried her right with him! 'Me, too.'

'I'll see you tomorrow.' The streak of dull colour highlighted the slashing high curve of his cheekbones.

'Early…*Please.*'

He looked startled and then pleased as his warm laughter welled. 'Tom's spending tomorrow with Tara before she flies back to Paris.'

'And her lover?'

Niall nodded. 'It's Fiona's day off, so tomorrow morning I'm a nanny-free, Tom-free zone…' His secretary would have a fit when he asked her not to come in only hours after he'd begged her to spend her precious Sunday helping him work on the backlog. He cheerfully ignored the slight guilty twinge of his deeply ingrained work ethic.

'Sounds good to me.' Holly smiled as she felt the tension ease, but she couldn't totally dismiss the nagging doubts that still lingered. 'What would you do, Niall…?' She took a deep breath. 'What if Rowena doesn't want you to sleep with me?' she blurted out.

With a sinking heart she saw his warm eyes turn icy arctic blue. I had to go and spoil it, didn't I? she wailed inwardly.

It was a valid point, she told herself stubbornly, no matter what he said. What if he did have to choose between casual sex with me and a long and valued friendship with my sister? Rowena wouldn't do anything so crude but…She couldn't help torturing herself with this humiliating scenario.

'Rowena…Rowena? What the hell has it got to do with her?' he blasted, his eyes blazing. 'I'd be worried if *you* didn't want to sleep with me—but you do, don't you, Holly?'

Meeting his eyes, her need was suffocating. Her shoulders sagged weakly as surrender rushed through her body. 'Yes,' she agreed simply. 'I do, Niall.'

'So much it hurts,' he persisted.

'It does…' A thought struck her. 'Do you…?' she began hopefully, the idea of their shared frustration pleased her.

'Agony,' he confirmed drily. He sucked in his breath and the erratic pulse in his lean cheek began once more to throb. 'You don't need to look so pleased. I've got to see you tomorrow.'

'Why not tonight?' Holly suggested hopefully. She saw his expression and thought she might have been *too* eager. She wasn't really keeping him guessing by giving the impression she'd be quite happy if he picked her up and tucked her under his arm. Perhaps he was one of those men she'd read about in the women's magazines, the ones who preferred the chase to the capture?

'As tempting as that idea is, I think you should go back in and find out what's bothering Rowena.' Being unselfish and noble wasn't all it was cracked up to be; he felt bloody awful!

Holly swallowed her disappointment. 'I think it's far more likely she'd confide in you.'

'Rowena doesn't have many friends, Holly.'

Holly thought of her sister's wide and extensive circle and gaped at him.

He read her incredulity. 'I mean *real* friends.'

There was only one friend she begrudged Rowena. 'She's got you.'

His expression was cold and unfriendly as his eyes swept over her face. 'It's a two-way thing, Holly. You expect me to fit in around your career, which you've made pretty clear comes first for you—'

It would seem that her efforts to paint herself as a career girl who would not only never seek to become emotionally dependent upon him, but would actively discourage such a situation, had been a bit too successful! Holly was startled to realise that he'd interpreted her often defensive comments as some sort of inflexible set of ground rules. There was nothing she'd like better than to combine marriage with a career, but she couldn't really contradict him now without doing some uncomfortable explaining.

'And I accept that.'

There was no mistaking the harsh resentment in his voice. For the first time, Holly wondered whether she'd actually been saying what he wanted to hear after all; she shook her head, dismissing the notion as fanciful.

'But there are some things *you* have to accept,' he added grimly as she tried to collect her confused thoughts. 'I'm thirty-one, Holly. I've got a lot of friends; I've got an ex-wife, a son, a family, a job—none of that is going to change dramatically because I've added a redhead to the list of things in my life. If you can ask me to turn my back on my friends, how long,' he enquired in a disillusioned voice, 'before you ask me to give up on my son? I couldn't…' He clung angrily to this certainty, while he was being torn to pieces by the devastating knowledge of how much he would be prepared to compromise his life to keep this woman in it. The completely uncharacteristic way he was prepared to play hooky the next morning was only a symptom of something much bigger.

'I'd never!' Holly cried in horror.

Stony-faced, he didn't respond to her exclamation. 'Think about it.'

He didn't add, if you don't like it, *tough*—but he might just as well have; his expression said as much, loud and clear!

Holly watched him disappear into the lift. She was pretty sure she'd think about what he'd said most of the night.

CHAPTER NINE

'I WASN'T sure if you'd come.' Dressed in an open-necked polo shirt and jeans, Niall stood to one side to let her enter the hallway. He sounded terse as opposed to bothered by her tardiness, and his expression gave no clue to the fact he'd been pacing the floor restlessly for the past hour.

'I wasn't sure if you still wanted me to,' she responded awkwardly.

Nostrils flared he gave a sceptical snort. 'I find that hard to believe.'

Flustered by not just his cryptic words but his mere magnetic presence, Holly looked around. The period hallway was dripping with the sort of original features that always featured prominently in any sales literature—not that this address would be hard to sell. Detached houses overlooking the park like this one were gobbled up by those lucky enough to be able to afford the prices they fetched.

'I didn't actually know where you lived—' she unwrapped the vividly patterned silk scarf from around her neck and held in uncertainly in her hand '—which sort of brought home to me how untraditional our...' She fumbled for words to describe what they had.

'Courtship is?' he suggested, entering the sunny living room at the back of the house behind her.

Holly's mouth was still open as, startled at his choice of word, she swung around to stare at him warily. His blue eyes held a very intense expression that made her over-sensitive stomach muscles quiver and melt into a pool of liquid warmth. Courtship bestowed something…what did it bestow? An aura of semi-permanence? Niall's expression didn't give much away, except perhaps he was feeling almost as wary as she was.

'That's one word for it,' she babbled, trying to cover the tense expectant pause. 'Do you like it?' She flicked her wrist and let the scarf drift out towards him. 'A present from Rowena. It's a…actually, I've forgotten, but it's a famous name,' she finished vaguely. Rowena had made a point of stressing that this wasn't some piece of tat to be treated casually—Holly's careless attitude to her possessions was a source of great irritation to her sister.

Niall caught the scarf, saying absently, without even looking at it, 'It's very pretty.' He tugged and Holly let the scarf slip through her fingers.

He might not be looking at the scarf, but he was looking at her—looking in the sort of way that sent her overheated blood pulsating full throttle around her tense body. Still without looking away, he draped the scarf carelessly over the small walnut bureau beside the fireplace.

'I'm not in the phone book. How did you get the address?'

'A quick trawl through Rowena's personal organiser. Because,' she added defensively, before he had time to condemn her furtive tactics, 'I could hardly ask her where you lived, could I? It's very nice here,' she added with an appreciative sigh as she walked over to French doors which opened out onto a pretty leafy garden that stretched impressively into the distance.

'The garden's one of the reasons I bought this place. A child needs a garden, and there's a good school nearby.'

And Niall, as the caring responsible parent he was, would think about such things. She admired these caring qualities he displayed where his son was concerned. The real man she'd got to know was a million miles away from the celebrity playboy the media liked to portray. If he ever did decide to commit again to a woman, she knew instinctively that he'd do it wholeheartedly. She knew he'd never do it at all until he got over his failed marriage to Tara, and maybe even Tara herself?

I have to be realistic, she told herself, stifling a forlorn sigh. That time might never come, and if it does I'll probably be long off the scene. She was destined to be a short interlude in his life and it would only hurt more if she let herself pretend otherwise. Unexpectedly, her eyes filled up; blinking back the hot sting, she lowered her gaze self-consciously from his disturbingly intent scrutiny.

'I think maybe we'd all, child or not, benefit from a garden,' she mused gruffly. 'There's something about a bit of green. I must remember to put a window-box on my list. I would have been here earlier,' she explained, 'only the landlord replied to the message I left. I've been looking at a flat.'

Even before this morning's experience, she hadn't felt upbeat about the chances of matching her inclinations to her budget—now she knew she'd have to lower her standards. Sharing was probably the best idea but, after years of sharing grotty student accommodation, she enjoyed her privacy. Oh, well, she reflected practically, it's all about compromise.

'Not good?'

'It smelt of cabbage.'

The line permanently etched between Niall's dark brows deepened. 'I thought Rowena wasn't back for good for a while yet. You two haven't…?'

'Come to blows over you, and I've been kicked out into the August snow?' she suggested, childishly jubilant that for once she was the one able to anticipate his thought!

'Sorry to disappoint you, Niall, but you hardly came up in the conversation,' she told him breezily.

She decided she wasn't going to mention the bit when she'd closed the subject on Niall by saying, 'he's my mistake to make, Rowena.' With the emphasis on 'mine'!

'If you discount the part where Rowena warned me you get bored easily...' Her voice suggested she found Rowena's point of view amusing. 'No, it's just never too early to start looking.'

'Bored!' Niall's smile flashed white and extremely attractive. 'She really doesn't know you very well, does she?'

'I think that was a compliment?' she quizzed him.

'It was.'

Holly nodded slowly. The morning was looking up, she decided cautiously. 'Just so long as I know.'

'If you're in any doubts, feel free to ask.'

'You were right about Rowena.'

'When you come to know me better,' he told her gravely, 'you'll come to appreciate the fact that I'm *always* right.'

His nonsense lightened the worried expression on her face for a moment. 'She got drunk after you'd gone.' She could see immediately that Niall appreciated, perhaps more than she did, just how uncharacteristic this behaviour was.

'Rowena?'

'Not fall down staggering drunk, you understand,' she hastened to assure him. 'More maudlin, where-is-my-life-going sort of drunk. I never knew,' she marvelled with transparent naiveté, 'that Rowena ever had any doubts. She always seemed to know exactly what she wants. I think it's all got something to do with Quinn Tyler.' She shook her head thoughtfully. Yeah, the more she thought about...'She didn't say anything specific, but his name came up a lot. You don't look surprised,' she accused. 'Is that why you had such a down on him? Did you know?'

Niall shrugged. 'I saw Quinn leaving Rowena's late one night, a while back. She tried to cover it up but she'd obviously been crying. He's got a reputation...'

'So have you,' she reminded him tartly. It hadn't escaped her notice he didn't offer any explanation of what he'd been doing at Rowena's *late*. 'And you made me cry, last night.' She shrugged. 'Does that make you a bad guy?'

Niall's big body went rigid; his eyes darkened dramatically. The only time he'd ever seen even a gleam of moisture in Holly's eyes was after they'd listened to a particularly sloppy piece of Puccini. Tough, self-reliant, stubbornly prosaic Holly crying...Something deep inside him rebelled fiercely at the idea.

'Probably.' She didn't notice his deep voice sounded oddly uneven and more gravelly than usual. 'You cried?'

Quite suddenly, he knew that he'd do just about anything to protect her from a potentially painful situation...and he'd been the one who made her cry! He took a deep shuddering breath, his nostrils flaring with self-disgust.

'I do, you know—cry, that is. Though—' she smiled a bit uncertainly up at him, but he didn't respond; his expression was oddly wooden, his normally mobile mouth set in a grim straight line '—not excessively.' His jaw, always firm, looked pretty uncompromising.

Niall cleared his throat before he eventually responded. 'I shouldn't have said...I didn't mean to make you cry.' His grim gaze seemed to be fixed at some point over her left shoulder.

'I know that, but you were quite right. I've been thinking about what you said. We both have our own lives to live. Just because we're lovers doesn't give me some sort of exclusivity deal…I know…'

That focused his attention with a vengeance. She took an instinctive step backwards as the laser intensity of his menacing blue glare hit her head-on.

He grabbed her shoulders firmly to stop further retreat. 'In my bed, it does!' he ground out.

His fingers bit hard into the soft flesh of her upper arms. It registered in her bemused brain that he was acting as if somehow she'd just mortally offended him.

'You may not be wearing my ring for real—'

'I'm not wearing it at all.' She held up her naked hand to prove the point.

'But I don't want to be one of many. There's a hell of lot of difference between casual and promiscuous.'

'I wasn't advocating bed-hopping,' she gasped, blushing wildly. 'I meant f-friendships, other commitments and so forth,' she stammered huskily. 'Actually, though, I'm quite glad you brought up the subject.' She certainly hadn't expected him to and definitely not in such an emphatic and spectacular manner! It would seem she had no worries on that score. 'I don't want to be your Friday girl or whatever…The one you fit in between—'

'The other members of my vast harem.'

She felt his body relax as his grip on her shoulders loosened. The tautness was still there, stretching the skin tight across his jutting, strong cheekbones, and that little nerve was still doing a war-dance in his lean cheek, but he no longer looked as if he was about to explode.

'Girl Friday?' One corner of his mouth quivered. He reached forwards and tucked a shiny strand of hair behind her ear. 'I've never been one for juggling,' he told her gravely. 'Besides, you're a high-maintenance sort of girlfriend. I don't think I'd have the time…' His dry humour seemed distinctly frazzled around the edges.

'I was thinking more about the inclination.' Holly, her confidence soaring, was beginning to enjoy herself. Niall wanted her and nobody else—at least for the moment.

Niall laughed and the remainder of the dangerous, explosive quality left his face. 'You're worried about my low boredom threshold?' His wry expression suggested he found the idea deeply amusing. 'If I live to be a hundred, you'd never bore me, little witch,' he told her, framing her face between his big hands. 'And you can quote me on that if you like.' His scrutiny held a heart-stopping degree of tender amusement.

Holly smiled back in what she suspected was a besotted sort of way at him. Suddenly she didn't care about hiding the way she felt. He was bound to find out eventually, she decided fatalistically—why not now? Not that she was going to blurt it out, or anything, but if he caught on, would it really matter…?

'Do people quote you often?' she enquired wonderingly. 'You know, Niall, I'm beginning to worry about your aspirations in the divine direction.'

'Shut up,' he advised benignly, just before he kissed her.

Holly tingled from the crown of her burnished head to her toes and all the places in between. *Only a kiss*, she thought wonderingly as he finally lifted his head. Whoever said that had definitely not been kissed by Niall Wesley! She clung to him for support and brought her forehead to rest against his chest.

'You're a very excellent kisser.' She lifted her head, looking slightly sheepish. 'And you can quote me on that,' she told him with the beginning of a smile.

Niall caught his breath; he fought a tough internal battle to maintain control. He'd been seduced on several occasions, often by women who were experts at the craft, but never so completely as with that not-quite smile. It was that sort of smile and this was the sort of feeling—the one like a dull knife in his guts—that men had been prepared to fight dragons and wage wars for down the years.

'I didn't think you were ever going to get around to it.' Her smile grew smugly satisfied as she looped her arms around his neck.

Her natural optimism was reasserting itself. This morning hadn't gone at all as she'd thought it would. She had imagined that Niall, like herself, would have spent the previous night realising that their relationship was doomed—they had nothing whatever in common. Rowena might not have dwelt on her sister's new and surprising relationship, but with a few well-chosen words she had managed to nurture the seeds of doubt that were already in Holly's mind after Niall's cryptic parting shot—it had sounded very like an ultimatum.

'But then that's why you asked me to come, isn't it?' she reminded him huskily.

He stiffened. She knew straight off she'd said the wrong thing; if she had any doubts, the cold disdain etched on his face didn't leave much room for doubt on that score. She just couldn't imagine what it was she'd done to anger him. Confusingly Niall, who had put the 'laid' into laid-back, seemed to have suddenly got awfully sensitive. Or was he, despite his reassurances to the contrary, just simply having doubts about the way things were going?

His hands went to hers, which still lay at the base of his skull and he brought them around to shoulder height.

'Sorry I didn't wade right into the foreplay, or did you want to skip that, too?' he enquired crudely. 'I mean, I can see it must be frustrating for you if I actually want to have a conversation first.'

'I don't believe this,' she gasped, her eyes widening to their fullest extent. 'You're actually accusing *me* of using *you* as a sex object! *Excuse me,*' she snapped, trying to pull her wrists from his grip, 'while I choke on the hypocrisy in the air. When have you treated me like anything else but a body?' This wasn't strictly true, but it was worth the lie to see his colour deepen significantly.

'I mean, what else would you want me for?' She looked expectantly towards him and for one moment it seemed as if he would reply to her jibe. Holly swallowed her disappointment when he maintained his silence and embraced her growing anger. 'You're the one who asked me to come here, and it wasn't to play dominoes!' she reflected bitterly.

A rumble emerged from Niall's throat that sounded surprisingly like laughter, but when she glared suspiciously at him his expression was as sober and earnest as she could have wished.

'Am I supposed to wait for you to make the first move? Well, in case you didn't notice, I did! Is it my fault I feel impatient? Is it my fault I want to rip your clothes off the instant I see you?' Holly tilted her head back and closed her eyes. It was too much to hope I only thought that. She opened one eye and risked a quick look. Oh, no, I said it, all right—from the expression on his face, I probably bellowed it!

Niall had brought her hands down, but he still hadn't released her, even though she'd tried to twist away. A dark corner to hide her terminal embarrassment seemed like an appealing option just now.

His thumbs began to rub the blue-veined inner aspect of her delicate-boned wrists. Tiny, tingling quivers of pleasure went zinging through her body. Holly tried to cling to the shreds of her hostility, but it was swallowed up by the insidious, soothing lethargy his touch induced.

'Can you actually play dominoes?'

She opened her heavy eyes and languidly lifted her head. 'I'm a legend at the local, back home.' It was impossible not to respond to the beguiling smile in his eyes.

'Perhaps you could teach me a few tricks?'

'Maybe…' she conceded with a sniff.

'The difficulty is, we spend most of our time together in bed… Not the place, I'm sure you agree, for domino lessons. If we spent more time together, it might be easier. If you moved in here, we'd have more time; I might even be able to teach you to cook.'

'You can cook?' Holly selected the less compelling and safer of the two questions she ached to ask. Her head was spinning. She was suffering from a heavy dose of unreality.

'Compared to you, I can cook.' Holly could only stare warily as he pulled out the stool set by the gleaming baby grand and casually straddled it. He patted the seat in front of him suggestively. 'You look as if you should sit down.'

She swallowed hard, and shook her head. Her heart was kicking wildly against her ribs. It was hard enough thinking on the opposite side of the room; if she settled in that comfortable spot between his legs, her intellect would go the same way as her morals and common sense.

'Did you just ask me to move in with you?' She laughed weakly to show she recognised a joke when she heard one.

Niall folded his arms across his chest and fixed his unblinking enigmatic stare upon her face. 'I did,' came the flat response.

'Oh!' she faltered hoarsely. 'This is pretty…pretty…'

'Unexpected?'

'I wish you'd stop doing that,' she rounded on him.

'Doing what?'

'Putting words in my mouth.'

'All right,' he acceded casually. 'There are other things I prefer to put in your mouth.' The gleam in his eyes deepened as she let out an inarticulate, shocked whimper. 'What were *you* going to say?'

He knew full well she couldn't say anything at all. Holly gritted her teeth. 'I was going to say, this is pretty sudden.'

'That puts a whole new perspective on things,' he agreed mockingly. 'What do you think about my idea?'

'You want the truth?'

'That depends on your answer.'

She frowned critically at his flippancy—this was no joking matter. 'You *really* want me to move in with you…?' She still couldn't quite believe he meant it. The cool, almost clinical expression on his face didn't suggest he was inspired by some wild romantic impulse—I should be so lucky, she thought. 'What would people say?'

'Do you care?' he wondered scornfully, dismissing public opinion with a careless flick of his elegant wrist.

Staring at his long, shapely, tapering fingers, she decided it was likely the piano wasn't just for show. She could see those hands moving over the keyboard—just thinking about how sensitive and skilful they were intensified the aching empty feeling low in her belly. Getting orgasmic about his hands—how hopeless is that? she despaired.

'I care about what some people think…My mum, my dad…'

'Your great-aunt and those two cousins twice removed, I know…and your pet rabbit is very sensitive about change, too,' he cut in impatiently. 'I asked what *you* thought, Holly. I think that's the important thing here.'

'Well, I'm not entirely sure what I think,' she hedged, 'until you tell me why you asked me.'

'I asked you because we're so sexually compatible it's off whatever scale these things are measured by...'

'That's not a reason to move in with someone,' she interrupted hoarsely. Did he really think that...? He *sounded* as though he did. Even though she craved a bit of depth in his feelings, his heartfelt fervour was extremely gratifying.

'It's one *great* reason,' he contradicted her firmly. 'But hold on; I've only just started. There's more. I just find when I'm in the same room as you, or even,' he added, making a clean breast of his dilemma, 'when I'm not, I tend to focus on that aspect quite a lot. But we have a lot of things going for us I could focus on.'

He thinks about me like I think about...Holly's breath seemed to burn as she forced herself to exhale slowly. Her eyes were dramatically dark and burning in her milk-pale face. She felt weak with desire...*And he hasn't even touched me!*

'I don't think you've thought this through, Niall.' One of them had to be practical.

'I've thought about very little else, Holly.' The words emerged almost reluctantly and his blue eyes blazed with similar angry resentment, mingled with something primal and raw.

Holly felt as if she were suffocating; she lowered her eyes abruptly.

'And if we're talking practical, Holly, what could be more practical than you moving in here? Would you prefer to end up sharing a house with strangers, or settling for some poky little bedsit that smells of cabbage? I wouldn't expect you to look after Tom, if that's what's bothering you, and you'd like Fiona, the nanny.'

'It's nothing to do with Tom,' she told him with a frown.

'You work long hours; here, you wouldn't have to come

home and start cooking and cleaning. My housekeeper lives in the flat over the garage; the place runs like clockwork.'

'Stop!' she pleaded sharply, holding up her hand. 'You don't have to sell the house, Niall—just your reasons for wanting me here.'

'You work long unsocial hours; so do I.'

'That's true,' she agreed.

'I want more than a few snatched hours with you.'

'*You do?*'

'You look shocked.'

'I am. Fall in a heap sort of shocked.'

'Is it a crime to want more?' he demanded angrily. 'I know your independence is important to you, but what we have isn't enough for me.' His dark brows drew together to form a dark uncompromising line as he glared at her with an if-you-don't-like-it-tough, sort of expression.

Holly was drowning in a flood of panic and desire. 'I suppose…' Her voice sounded echoey and distant. 'We'd find out soon enough if boredom was going to set in.' The whole scenario had a strange dreamlike quality.

'I've already told you I'll never—'

'I was thinking more about you boring me, actually…'

Niall shot to his feet. All that was lacking was a victorious war cry; he positively oozed male triumph. 'That's settled, then!'

'Is this the point where we spit on our hands and shake?' she enquired tremulously. He hadn't said he loved her, not even once. But then Niall was a pretty straight-talking sort of man; he wouldn't insult her by faking it. 'I'll pass, if you don't mind.'

The basic need to conquer and master was buried deep in most males, no matter how superficially civilised they were. In some, she reflected, looking at Niall's tall, commanding figure, it was hardly buried at all! For a vanquished party, she felt pretty damned good. For a man like Niall to suggest they move in together, his feelings obviously ran deeper than he was admitting—maybe not the L word, but maybe deeper than he actually knew. If she was patient and didn't push it, she thought exuberantly…who knows?

Niall stretched out his hand and Holly automatically did the same. 'I was thinking of an exchange of bodily fluids,' he admitted, straight-faced. 'Just not that one,' he explained outrageously.

Instead of shaking her hand, he grabbed her wrist and yanked her, sending her on a collision course with his chest. His strong arms cushioned the impact but not the flood of desire that made her cling weakly to him.

His lean fingers twisted in her bright hair and he dragged her head backwards. 'Open your mouth, Holly,' he commanded urgently. 'I want to taste you. Sweet…sweet… Holly…'

Holly touched the tip of her tongue thoughtfully to her upper lip. 'You make me sound cloying and sickly.'

The wilful little pout made his breathing quicken. 'Honeyed and luscious,' he corrected throatily; he was looking with unambiguous hunger at the modest but very inviting swell of her breasts. His stark expression wiped the flirtatious look off her face.

'I can live with that,' she conceded huskily.

'And me?' One dark slanted brow quirked.

'Time will tell.'

Niall looked exasperated by her cautious response. Her lips parted under the forceful pressure of his lips. She twisted sinuously as his hands began to move over her body.

'Well, we've got plenty of that, anyhow. Time…' he

reminded her, in response to her glazed uncomprehending stare. 'Tom's staying with Tara tonight.'

'Well, actually, Niall…'

'You don't start work until Monday, do you?'

'It's not that. It's just Rowena seemed so low and I…I sort of suggested we all go out to dinner tonight…She's flying out…What are you doing?' she gasped, as he swung her up into his arms.

'I'm not wasting any time is what I'm doing,' he told her, striding purposefully out of the room. 'The guided tour of your new home. I think we'll start with the bedroom.'

'Excellent idea,' she approved.

He never did get around to showing her the rest of the house.

CHAPTER TEN

HOLLY was awoken from a deep sleep by the insistent sound of the door being hammered. She switched on the bedside light and brushed aside the clinging shreds of sleep.

She glanced at the clock. Had Rowena missed her flight? Wistfully, she looked towards the empty pillow beside her. It shouldn't have been empty, but Niall had left when they were halfway through their meal in response to an SOS from Tara.

Niall hadn't seem overly concerned by the news Tom was being violently sick—or, for that matter, particularly surprised. He explained that Tara was a soft touch where their son was concerned and, being a small boy, Tom took advantage and pigged out big time on junk food if he got the opportunity.

Holly hadn't worried much about his departure until Rowena had remarked how much she would hate to have a man who dropped everything at the behest of his ex-wife. She had managed to imply that she wouldn't be content with playing second fiddle. Holly had *tried* not to brood over Rowena's comments. Rowena was pretty poisonous where Tara was concerned—a prime example of her self-confessed territorial instincts at work? She found herself wondering how her own relationship with Niall would stand up to the pressure if Rowena started getting territorial.

Perhaps, Holly speculated, hurriedly drawing on a light

summer wrap, Tom had staged a miraculous recovery. Her heart began to race in eager anticipation.

She opened the door and her visitor almost fell over the door step.

'Where is she?' The visitor demanded belligerently. He staggered backwards and leant heavily against the wall to steady himself while he worked on the awkward problem of moving forwards once more.

'Quinn…?' Holly trotted after him as he stalked unsteadily into the open plan living area.

'I know she's back…She's been seen. Don't bother trying to deny it.'

The Quinn Tyler she knew was a tall, strikingly confident individual with a penchant for exquisitely cut expensive suits, girls with long legs and, if the rumours were true, fast motorbikes. She was sure he would look stunning in his biker leathers—tonight, he didn't look stunning, he looked ravaged.

The stubble on his square jaw was too abundant to be termed designer anything and his green eyes were red-rimmed and bloodshot. His suit was crumpled past redemption and he reeked of booze. If she hadn't known him, she might have crossed to the opposite side of the street if she'd seen him coming; there was a palpable air of barely repressed violence about him.

The startling transformation from sleekly urbane professional to drunken wreck was remarkable enough to make Holly stare and continue to stare as he started looking behind chairs, even inside cupboards, in his search for Rowena. It was interesting to note that even inebriated he was meticulously methodical, if not altogether practical in his approach.

'I know you're here,' he slurred at regular intervals.

'Quinn, I think you should sit down…' She stopped.

Maybe not; if he sat down, she wasn't sure she'd be able to get him up again. 'You can't go—' she began in alarm as he lurched towards the bedroom. Quinn, it seemed, wasn't in a listening mood.

She winced as the door hit the bedroom wall with a massive thud that reverberated through the entire flat. What Rowena would say about a great hole in her plaster— Quinn was a big man—God alone knew, she fretted, following him.

'Oh, God, where is she?' The big bad man had turned abruptly into the little boy.

Holly was too horrified to be beguiled by the transformation. He was lying full-length on the bed she'd just vacated.

'I know she's here somewhere. I can smell her,' he insisted, lifting a pillow to his face and inhaling deeply. 'It's still warm. The bed's still warm...Holly.'

'She's flown back to New York, Quinn,' Holly told him gently. Her soft heart oozed compassion as she knelt on the edge of the bed and looked down at the pitiful figure he made.

'I don't believe you.'

'I wouldn't lie to you, Quinn.'

'No, you're a nice girl, Holly,' he slurred sentimentally. 'Why didn't I fall for a nice girl like you? A reasonable girl. I'm not unreasonable, am I?' He grabbed her hand and appealed to her.

'You're drunk, Quinn.'

'Plastered,' he agreed gravely. 'Off my head, drunk as skink...skunk. What should I do, Holly? P-pretty name, Holly. I like it.'

'Thank you.' She wondered whether he'd remember any of this tomorrow, and hoped for both of their sakes he didn't. 'Go home and sleep it off.' She patted his shoulder consolingly.

He blinked owlishly up at the ceiling. 'Excellent idea. The thing is, I don't actually think I can move,' he grimaced apologetically and looked down at his uncooperative limbs.

Holly sighed heavily. Short of acquiring heavy lifting gear, what alternative did she have? 'You'd better stay here.'

'Make some man a great wife,' Quinn murmured, closing his eyes. 'Extremely grateful,' he added with exquisite politeness. About twenty seconds elapsed before he started snoring.

Out for the count! Holly stared at his unconscious figure with amused irritation. *Men!* Tutting quietly to herself, she unlaced and pulled off his shoes, removed his tie and loosened his shirt. With a sigh, she removed a pillow from the other side of the bed for herself and used the others to prop the big man up on his side in the recovery position. If he did throw up, he could forget about getting together with Rowena; her sister was extremely squeamish, not to mention intolerant, about such things. She unfolded the foldaway bed she'd used while Rowena was here and made up a bed.

Holly was folding the put-you-up away the next morning when Quinn finally surfaced. Amazingly—she'd deliberately let out all the stops when rendering her off-key version of a popular tune—he'd managed to sleep solidly through her noisy occupation of the shower room. He sat up, looked at her with a comically startled expression, and then, clutching his head, fell back down, groaning.

'Oh, God!' he groaned. 'I'm dying.'

'I shouldn't think so.'

'Holly?' Sitting up, cautiously this time, Quinn looked at her through eyes slitted against the light in the room. She saw in his eyes the moment when he remembered. 'Holly!' he groaned.

'You remember last night?'

'Most of it,' he agreed warily. 'I didn't do anything— make a nuisance of myself—did I?' He rubbed his head gingerly, making his brown hair stand spikily on end.

'Discretion is my middle name,' she assured him soothingly. 'Though it might be an idea if you got someone to do something about the chunk of plaster you knocked out of the wall. Rowena's rather particular about that sort of thing.'

At the mention of her sister, Quinn's expression got all mean and broody. What, Holly couldn't help but wonder, would have happened if Rowena had been here last night?

'I'll do that. I'm sorry I stole your bed last night.' He was looking with some concern at her light robe.

Holly's lips quivered. 'Yes, you did,' she reassured him. 'You're not my type, Quinn.'

The big man looked sheepish but, encouraged by the twinkle in her eyes, eventually grinned. 'Yes, well…' He grimaced. 'God, but my mouth tastes disgusting.'

'Shower and toothpaste are at your disposal.'

'You're an angel,' he breathed gratefully. 'You wouldn't have such a thing as an aspirin, would you…?'

'Better make it paracetemol, considering the condition of your poor abused stomach-lining. I'll put on the coffee.'

'Thanks, Holly,' he said quietly as she turned to leave.

'For the coffee?'

'That and not asking questions.'

The coffee was brewing nicely when she heard the post clunk on the carpet, followed by a polite tap on the door.

'Niall!' She gaped at the tall figure who handed her a small parcel. 'What are you doing here?'

Niall planted his hands firmly about her waist, his lips firmly on her mouth and walked into the flat, kicking the door shut behind him. He smelt sexily wholesome, all squeaky freshly washed hair and warm male. Holly sighed with pleasure and kissed him back with enthusiasm.

'We need to talk.'

'Fine,' she agreed, not understanding the air of tension he was exuding. 'Is Tom better?' she murmured, planting a couple of small kisses against his lean cheek. She trailed a finger down his jawline as he placed her back on her feet.

'Right as rain.' He turned his head and kissed the tip of her finger. His hot summer sky eyes moved greedily over her face and flickered with interest towards the loose neck of her wrap. Holly felt her stomach muscles spasm.

'What did you want to talk about?'

His eyes shifted from hers evasively. 'I wanted to wish you luck.' Spineless coward, he told himself scornfully.

'Is that all?'

'First day in your new job. Have you forgotten, or are you just super-cool and confident?'

'I wish.' Why did she get the impression he was avoiding saying something?

'Mmm, that smells good.' His elegant nose twitched appreciatively. 'Are you nervous?' His expression became concerned.

Nervous...You could say that. Why hadn't it occurred to her until this second how this perfectly innocent situation might be misinterpreted? She couldn't help her glance flickering nervously towards the bedroom door.

'A bit,' she agreed, watching Niall's narrowed gaze automatically following the direction of her eyes. 'The thing is, I didn't get much sleep last night.' Best to get the explanations out of the way now.

'Lead me to the coffee.' Quinn, bare-chested and rubbing his wet hair on a towel, walked into the room. 'Just what the doctor ordered...' He saw Niall and stopped, looking self-conscious. 'Niall, this is a surprise.' From his tone, it was pretty obvious it wasn't a pleasant one.

'For you and me both, mate, friend, buddy, old pal...' Niall's icy contemptuous drawl made Holly wince and Quinn frown in genuine bewilderment. 'Holly's just been telling me she didn't get much sleep last night.'

'I'm afraid,' Quinn said apologetically, 'that's my fault.'

Holly groaned. How, she wondered, had Quinn failed to see the very obvious danger signs? Niall was simply oozing suspicion and antagonism.

'Niall, this isn't—' She made a desperate, last-ditch attempt to nip this farcical situation in the bud.

'What it looks like?' Niall gave an ugly laugh, took one step forwards and launched a vicious jab that landed on the jaw of the other man who, taken off guard and still feeling distinctly fragile, staggered backwards until he hit the wall and then gracefully slid down it.

Holly flew forward to catch an odd, squiggly shaped piece of pottery that Rowena had proudly explained was by one of the most collectable young potters in the country; she was too late. She moaned as she watched the investment shatter on the floor.

She stamped her small foot and glared at Niall. 'Now look what you've done!' she wailed furiously.

'Pity you didn't show the same respect for the rest of Rowena's property.' With a contemptuous curl of his lips Niall jerked his head sharply in Quinn's direction. 'You really have come out of her shadow with a vengeance, haven't you?' he jeered.

Holly felt her temper flare as she registered the sordid insinuation that she'd sleep with her sister's man as part of some sick game of one-upmanship. Was that what he thought of her? she wondered sickly.

Just when she thought he'd insulted her as much as he could, he came up with an even more unsavoury interpretation.

'Or had this been a long-term arrangement? If I'd known you wanted a relationship that doesn't extend beyond the bedroom, it would have made life a lot easier.'

'I've no desire to make your life easy!' she yelled back.

'Tell me something I didn't know already. You've done nothing but turn my life upside down since the moment you insinuated yourself—'

'Insinuated!' She gaped at him with raw incredulity— was he *serious*? 'I didn't do any insinuating. It was against my better judgement that I helped you...and,' she spat venomously, 'I wish I hadn't.'

'Always was a grotesque piece of tat,' Quinn mumbled, looking in a dazed fashion at the broken shard of pottery. He reached up to gingerly feel his rapidly swelling lip.

The unexpected sound of Quinn's voice acted like a cattle-prod on Niall, who had in the heat of battle forgotten his adversary; he bristled, the aura of violence about him deepening perceptively.

'Who the hell cares?' he flared, his eyes blazing contempt. 'Get up, Tyler!' His searing glare switched back to Holly. 'And don't expect me to buy any stories about last night being the first time.'

'It wasn't.' She threw him a haughty pitying glance. Not the first, second or last, you *stupid* man, she thought furiously.

Niall's fists tightened until each clenched knuckle individually cracked. His eyes had all the warmth of stones as he watched Holly worriedly bend over Quinn—his *friend* Quinn. Not only had she not bothered defending herself, she was actually flaunting the truth under his nose. The buzzing in his brain made it hard to think straight. All that stuff about Quinn and Rowena must have been a blind and, like a prize sucker, he'd fallen for it!

'Don't get up, Quinn,' Holly advised urgently. 'He'll only knock you down again.'

'Don't bet on it,' Quinn responded pugnaciously. 'He took me off guard.'

'There's one way to find out,' Niall goaded belligerently. 'Do you call her or does she call you?' he ground out from between clenched teeth. 'What do you call it? Being her mentor?'

'If I can't last the night without a man, you mean?' Holly hooted derisively. Men and their macho posturing, she thought, giving a delicate shudder of loathing. A life of celibacy looked all of a sudden very attractive!

'*Please* don't bleed on Rowena's carpet,' she beseeched as Quinn made an abortive attempt to rise. 'And for heavens's sake, Niall, stop glowering like that!' she rounded on him. 'You're making a complete fool of yourself,' she warned him bitterly.

'There's a lot of that in the air,' Quinn muttered, with a sudden surge of fellow-feeling for the man who'd knocked him down.

Niall didn't display any similar feelings of camaraderie as he rounded angrily on his contemporary. 'When I want your opinion, Tyler, I'll ask for it—only don't hold your breath. On second thoughts,' he snarled childishly, '*do*!'

'What do you sound like?' Hands on her hips, Holly divided her withering glance equally between the two men. 'For God's sake, grow up, the pair of you!'

Quinn reluctantly smiled as he struggled to his feet. 'Yes, ma'am.' He clutched his head in obvious discomfort.

'Well, you've only yourself to blame!' Holly told him callously, her sympathy sorely tried.

'That makes it worse.' Quinn confided.

'If you can't stand the pace, perhaps you should stay out of her bed.'

At this fresh slur, Holly caught her breath angrily. 'This has gone far enough, Niall. You're behaving like a jealous—'

Niall's eyes darkened; his body was rigid with barely contained fury. He'd make her want him so badly she'd beg and he'd just walk away—yes, that was what he would do, he brooded, gaining no comfort from his dark thoughts of revenge.

'Of course I'm jealous, woman!' he snarled contemptuously. 'What man wouldn't be, finding the woman he's stupid enough to love has just spent the night with a bed hopping Casanova!'

A silent implosion went off inside her skull. *'What did you say?'*

Niall's head snapped back, as if an invisible fist had just landed a blow dead centre. The dull slashes of high colour made his cheekbones seem more prominent.

'I said,' he ground out, in an obvious effort to distract and confuse the issue, 'I was going to spoil his pretty face.'

In Holly's admittedly biased opinion, Niall had a *much* prettier face. 'No, you didn't.'

'That's as maybe, but I am anyway,' he growled.

Quinn was looking from one to the other with a wry expression on his bruised face.

'Well, you know where to find me, Niall, if you feel the urge to do anything about it.' He ignored Niall's savage hiss as he bent to kiss Holly's cheek. 'Thanks, Holly…'

She was impressed he didn't recoil under the white-hot fury when he turned his head slowly to look directly at Niall. 'For giving up your bed for me.'

'Your shirt…jacket…' Holly mumbled, dashing back into the bedroom and returning with both. Hurry up… Hurry up, she silently urged him, bundling the garments into his arms.

'Where do you think you're going, Tyler?' Niall asked suspiciously.

'Home, mate,' Quinn informed him wearily. 'I'd invite you, but I suspect you've got better things to do.' He looked pretty pointedly at Holly.

He looked like hell, and Holly felt a spasm of guilt because she selfishly couldn't wait to see the back of him. She made a determined effort to compensate for her callous behaviour, although all she was actually conscious of was the anticipation growing inside her—he had said it, he really had—Niall loves me! She gloatingly luxuriated in the warm glow of this revelation as she touched Quinn's arm.

'You won't drive, will you, Quinn?' she fussed as he eased on his jacket.

'To tell you the truth, Holly, I've not the faintest idea where I left my car.' He reached into his jacket pocket. 'Or my wallet. I don't suppose you…?'

Holly extracted her purse from her shoulder-bag, which lay on the work counter, and handed him the small wad of notes from inside.

'I've said it before, you're an angel of mercy. I did say it, didn't I…?'

Holly grinned. 'Bye, Quinn.'

'Er, Holly, you won't mention this to…erm…anyone… will you?'

It didn't take a genius to work out who that particular anyone was. Holly nodded understandingly.

'You didn't answer my question, Niall,' she reminded him softly as the door clicked closed.

Niall started. 'What?'

'Don't play dumb. You heard.'

He'd have been blind not to see that nothing in that little interchange had said lovers. Niall swallowed; it was dawning on him that he had egg on his face in a big way!

'You didn't sleep with him last night, did you?'

Holly smiled righteously, enjoying his patent discomfort. He deserved to suffer...Had he really said what she'd thought he'd said...? The tight knot of excitement in her chest gave an odd fluttery feeling.

'Not ever?'

'You sound disappointed, as would I have been if I'd lusted after Quinn's body last night—he was comatose.'

'You must admit, it looked pretty bad,' he protested feebly.

'To someone who doesn't know what trust is,' she agreed with a sweet smile. 'Having a mind like a sewer probably helps, too.'

Niall ground his teeth. 'I just can't imagine anyone *not* wanting to sleep with you.'

'You can't?' she echoed, not unnaturally entranced by this point of view.

'You're the most beautiful, desirable woman I've ever seen.' His hungry eyes roamed restlessly over her face. 'I love you. I'm in love with you, Holly—have been almost from that first night.' His voice cracked. 'Although it took me a little while to catch on, myself, add up all the clues that kept hitting me in the face,' he rasped.

Holly could hardly credit that she—ordinary run-of-the-mill Holly—had aroused this depth of his feeling in a man like Niall Wesley.

'You've only known me a little time, Niall.'

Niall sighed heavily and brushed a hank of dark hair impatiently from his eyes. 'That's part of the problem, isn't it?'

Holly remained silent with difficulty. She didn't want to stop him mid-flow but from where she was standing there wasn't any problem at all! For the first time in what felt like a long long time, there wasn't a single cloud on her personal horizon.

'I knew it was too soon.' Niall shook his head morosely. 'People don't fall in love overnight.'

'You did, it would seem.' She couldn't resist the opportunity to hear him say it again. She felt light; flying, she reflected joyously, could not be more exhilarating than this!

'I did.' Niall gritted his teeth; his compelling gaze refused to release her. 'I know you're not in love with me,' he continued urgently. 'But you could be if you let yourself. We can go slowly...'

Holly lowered her eyes. 'I don't think so.'

The colour seeped from his skin, leaving an unhealthy grey sheen. 'I respect your career...' His voice was low and urgent as his hands curved tightly around her forearms. 'I've already got Tom; there would be no pressure to have a family. As for marriage...' His shoulders lifted expressively. 'What does a little piece of paper mean...?' he said without much conviction. 'I know I can make you happy if you let me!' he ground out fiercely.

If she'd let him! Holly felt tears of pure happiness well in her eyes. She sniffed them back. So, deep down, Niall Wesley was an old-fashioned sort of guy. Holly raised her still-swimming eyes and the sultry glow he saw there immobilised Niall.

'Don't give up your day job. As a salesman, you stink,' she told him huskily.

A glimmer of something like relief started to shine in his extraordinary eyes. 'Is that so?'

'I'm just not interested in the product you're selling.' Gravely she placed her hands along the sides of his face and gazed lovingly up into his face. 'I do want babies and the piece of paper—not necessarily in that order, you understand, and not immediately—I mean the baby bit, here.'

His old ruthless grin blazed out. 'And will just any old father do for these babies?'

Holly found she was happy to see his arrogant confidence back in place. 'I'm a bit choosy,' she confessed with a gusty sigh and let her hands slide all the way down his strong broad back until they came to rest with casual familiarity on the taut curve of his bottom. 'Trust would be important, of course—essential, actually…' she couldn't resist teasing.

'You hypocritical little wretch,' Niall cried out, kissing the provocative pout clear off her lips. 'I suppose if you'd discovered your sister or Tara walking half-naked out of my bedroom, you'd have been objective as hell!'

Holly chuckled, a delightfully rich wicked sound. 'I'd have killed you stone dead,' she confessed. 'I don't know which one I've been more jealous of…I mean, it's not as if I'm exactly a show stopper…' A troubled frown puckered her smooth brow.

'You're a heart-stopper,' he told her with unflinching conviction. 'At least, as far as my heart is concerned. I've never felt about anyone the way I feel about you. You do believe me, don't you?' His voice throbbed with emotion.

'Yes, oh, yes, Niall, and I feel that way too. Only you

can't blame me for wondering. You didn't say or even hint even once,' she protested.

'I asked you to move in with me,' he pointed out.

'For purely practical reasons.' His lecherous grin made her blush. 'Well, not quite entirely practical,' she conceded, 'but I know love didn't enter into the argument...Believe me, I'd have remembered,' she assured him drily.

'I wanted to show you I was that man prepared to wait for you.'

'Oh, Niall! That's the most romantic thing I've ever heard,' she sighed.

His broad shoulders lifted almost self-consciously. 'I have my moments. Unless he's a masochist, my love, a man doesn't tell a woman who goes out of her way to tell him that she's *not* in love with him that he's fallen hook, line and the proverbial sinker!'

'Say it again!' she insisted urgently.

'What?'

'My love...my love!' she parroted eagerly.

'My love,' he repeated obligingly.

Holly happily hooked her arms around his neck and squirmed as close as she could get to his body. 'You were the big cynic about love, marriage and all that sort of thing. The original once stung man!' she reminded him with a reproachful pout.

'I don't like failure,' he admitted, 'but that's as deep as it went for me with Tara. We were both too young and I, at least, was as shallow as hell. But we had Tom, so I can never regret that. Holly...?'

She responded to the unspoken question in his eyes hastily. 'I'd have to be pretty shallow myself, not to mention mean, to resent Tom, Niall. He's part of you, and,' she explained simply, 'I love you. You've no idea how good it feels to say that,' she breathed rapturously.

His eyes blazed. 'You've no idea,' he responded huskily, 'how good it feels to hear you say it.' His arms tightened around her narrow ribcage.

'I thought the quickest way to send you running for cover was to tell you I'd fallen in love.'

'For the short time I was in denial, you'd probably have been right,' he conceded with a self-derisive grimace. 'It's taken some time,' Niall conceded slowly, 'but I think I'm finally ready for a proper grown-up marriage. How about you?'

'I feel extremely grown-up,' she confessed.

'Hell, you look about eighteen,' he laughed. 'Thank God you're not!' he added with feeling.

'This isn't to be a marriage of convenience, then?' she teased.

'How's that?'

'Well, you must admit it will be very convenient not having to explain to your family that you've dumped me.'

'If you carry on looking at me like that, little one, I'll have to explain to them why we got married before they got back!'

You ain't seen nothing yet, she thought happily. 'Truly...?' she prompted with a sly sultry smile.

'Truly.' He produced a small velvet box from his pocket. 'Just on the off chance,' he explained glibly, 'I had this made smaller and never did put this back in the bank vault.' He slid the big sapphire on her finger.

'It's perfect.'

'No, you're perfect. Let's go and celebrate your perfection!' he enthused, sweeping her up into his arms.

'Oh, dear!' she groaned, burrowing her head against his chest. 'We can't...'

'Can't?'

'Not can't as in "don't want to",' she assured him with flattering frustration. 'Can't as in I'm on duty in forty minutes.'

With a rueful grin Niall set her back down on her feet. 'I suppose we might as well start as we mean to go on. This is going to happen a lot, isn't it?'

Holly tried to gauge his reaction. 'It is,' she confirmed unhappily. 'Do you mind?' she asked worriedly.

'Mind that I can't spend the morning and possibly the afternoon, too,' he added, making a lecherous inspection of the open neck of her robe, 'making love to you? Of course I mind! But, I'm not about to stamp my feet and ask you to choose between me and your work.' His expression tender, he took her chin in his hand. 'Give me some credit, Holly.'

'Sorry,' she whispered.

'You can have us both.'

How did I get this lucky? she wondered. 'If I did have to choose, Niall, I'd—'

He placed a finger to her lips. 'Do you think I don't know that, Holly?' There was a fiercely possessive gleam in his sky blue eyes. 'You know I won't be asking.'

Holly swallowed the emotional constriction in her throat. 'I know. Actually,' she began unsteadily, 'I could always be late…?'

Niall caught his breath at the slumberous desire gleaming in her sloe-dark eyes. There was nothing he'd like to do more than respond to that smoky invitation. There was an expectant pause. He pulled himself together and did the decent thing, even though it hurt like hell.

'On your first day? Shame on you, woman!' he chided. 'Get some clothes on before I dress you myself.' He aimed a firm hand at her rear.

Head on one side, she regarded him with smouldering eyes. 'How about if I dress myself now and you undress me tonight?'

Niall grinned. 'Done! So long as those stripy pyjamas aren't involved,' he added cautiously. 'One of these days, you've got to tell me who they belong to…' he brooded.

'One of these days, I will,' she agreed solemnly. 'If marriage is about compromise like this, I think I'm going to like it.'

'Oh, my darling, you are, I promise,' he rasped with husky sincerity.

Holly believed him.